THE LONGEST DANCE

Recent Titles by Cynthia Harrod-Eagles

A CORNISH AFFAIR *
DANGEROUS LOVE *
DIVIDED LOVE *
EVEN CHANCE *
LAST RUN *
THE LONGEST DANCE *
NOBODY'S FOOL *
ON WINGS OF LOVE *
PLAY FOR LOVE *
A RAINBOW SUMMER *
REAL LIFE (*Short Stories*) *

* *all available from Severn House*

The Bill Slider Series

ORCHESTRATED DEATH
DEATH WATCH
NECROCHIP (*USA Title:* DEATH TO GO)
DEAD END (*USA Title:* GRAVE MUSIC)
BLOOD LINES
KILLING TIME
SHALLOW GRAVE
BLOOD SINISTER

THE LONGEST DANCE

Cynthia Harrod-Eagles

This first world edition published in Great Britain 2000 by
SEVERN HOUSE PUBLISHERS LTD of
9–15 High Street, Sutton, Surrey SM1 1DF.
This first world edition published in the USA 2000 by
SEVERN HOUSE PUBLISHERS INC of
595 Madison Avenue, New York, N.Y. 10022.

British Library Cataloguing in Publication Data

Harrod-Eagles, Cynthia
The longest dance
1. Love stories
I. Title
823.9'14 [F]

ISBN 0-7278-5610-3

Typeset by Hewer Text Ltd.,
Edinburgh, Scotland.
Printed and bound in Great Britain by
MPG Books Ltd, Bodmin, Cornwall.

I have forgot much, Cynara! gone with the wind,
Flung roses, roses riotously with the throng,
Dancing, to put thy pale lost lilies out of mind;
But I was desolate and sick of an old passion,
  Yea, all the time, because the dance was long:
I have been faithful to thee, Cynara! in my fashion.

I cried for madder music and for stronger wine,
But when the feast is finish'd and the lamps expire,
Then falls thy shadow, Cynara! the night is thine;
And I am desolate and sick of an old passion,
  Yea, hungry for the lips of my desire:
I have been faithful to thee, Cynara! in my fashion.

Ernest Dowson: *Non sum qualis eram bonae sub regno Cynarae*

Prologue

And now there remained only to drive home. By car there was just one possible route, familiar now beyond thought, beyond irritation, done always in the dark and always in weariness.

The dark of the countryside terrified him. It was not the matt, known darkness of towns, the controllable darkness of one's own house. It was a living thing, a hostile, pulsing blackness that crouched just beyond the feeble circle of his headlamps, and raced behind his fleeing car, never quite catching it, never far behind.

The white gate jumped into his headlights from the left, and he gripped the wheel in a tired spasm to stop himself reacting. His eyesight was poor, though he would never admit it. Sometimes he had trouble reading scores if they were old, rubbed, pencil-marked. He practised more, holding the score close while he was alone, playing half from memory at the sessions. It seemed to him the last straw, the final burden he could not endure, to be cursed with bad sight. In the inarticulate recesses of his brain he feared that if he yielded to his myopia, admitted it, took to wearing glasses, he would go blind; so he lied and memorised.

His mind was fragmented with tiredness. Scraps of music, words, pictures fluttered like rubbish blowing along a gutter; thoughts sloughed off and rattled like dry leaves blown by a little wind. She had lifted her white arms, their tender flanks rounded and soft as water. "What have you been doing since I saw you last? Was it for this that we suffered?"

Endure. Live and endure had come to mean the same thing. On his left now appeared a dying tree, infected with Dutch elm disease, so that its afflicted limbs stuck up nakedly from the pubic bushiness of its lower branches. Would all the trees die, *all* of them? Every day there were more. Their slow deaths at every bend of the road filled him with horror: dreading to see them, they were all he saw. Fully leafed, the other trees merged unnoticed into the dark background of their naked deaths, obscene as a burnt house.

"What do you do now?"

"Oh, I endure." She had said that, not him. "Oh, I endure – and you?"

"I work," he had said.

"Then I envy you. Work is at least a constructive thing. Work is not labour. I merely endure."

"Oh, I work," he had said. Answered without thinking, a social answer. He had not wanted to think, for the thoughts that filled his head day after day were loud and defiant. The train had swayed, knocking and rattling, rubbing its disjointed length along an unevenness in the track; its noises were hollow from the inside, deafeningly important outside, like most conversation. He had swayed clumsily, banging against the partition, too tired to poise himself for the journey. And she had swayed too, but with more resilience; her bare arm brushed against him, and she righted herself, patiently.

Patient, pliant, she had righted herself, standing back from him the better to see him, and to him she was a little blurred.

His hands on the wheel were damp. There was a little ache in his back from sitting badly, and as he wriggled in the seat to inch himself straighter he felt his body swirl round him and settle again.

God in heaven, was it for this *that we suffered?* Not for any glory of a fighting death, not for the hope of winning, but for this soft, sweet, pulpy present, this effortless slither down the far side of exertion. He felt his body around him, not deformed or injured or grotesque, but merely soft, a softness covered in slackening skin. *When was the last time I had sex? When was the last time I worried about it? When was the last time I felt hungry or thirsty or tired – not this dead-weight weariness, but the opened-out tiredness of stretched muscles and a pounding heart?*

No more suffering now – I merely endure. The smell of his house – a warm, smeary smell of children and food. And the dog. His late-night walk with Judy had become the briefest possible tug to a tree to stand shivering, seeing nothing, pushing the dark aside with bulging, aching eyes, before dragging her back disappointed, poor bitch, into the fusty safety of the house. Only darkness and its terrors stood between him and blankness, rescued his personality from oblivion. Once he had been hard, and life hard inside him, keeping him taut; and, as if choice were unending riches, he had let her go.

But today, today . . . She had lifted her white arms in an uncompleted gesture, and he had stared at their curved flanks and felt his own body thick around him like quilting. Like the numbness after the sixth whisky, the thickness of the lips that won't form the words properly, the fumbling mind that won't think them properly. In whisky he found some kind of relief from the pain of feeling no pain, for its bitter, woody smell, its taste like leaves, were intimately of the past. No whisky was ever in the present. The taste and smell were the authentic stuff of nostalgia, with memory thick like lees in the bottom of each glass.

She had always been there, poised on the edge of his vision, not touching him, righting herself after each shock, more resilient than him, resilient and patient. She never touched the bar against which he leaned. She grew out of the bar floor like a tree, and the roof opened above her, drew back so as not to touch her branches. She walked dry-footed through the pools of spilt beer and rose unprofaned from sin. They had drunk whisky together in a hundred bars, and always in the past. Even now, when the smell of her was still in his nostrils, she was in the past. *Oh, dear God!*

"I envy you your work."

"My work stopped being creative years ago," he had said. Bitterly, he had discovered it. Life had become a battle to maintain what was, surely, almost without value. Struggle to cover up his defective sight; struggle not to drink too much, not to be caught in drink; struggle – this for him alone – to disguise the fact that there was darkness, inside and out. There was no more passion in him. He made music out of emptiness, hiding its emptiness with noise. Well, the orchestra wanted note-perfection, and that was a realistic struggle, a concrete, day-to-day thing, a feasible effort. A way to keep from thinking.

A long way away, distant and alone, his feet slowed the car. His remote hands changed gear, changed down again, and he turned the car into his own lane. A narrow, rutted lane, filled in spring with eddying clouds of elderflowers, in summer with high white dust. He did not know how he had got here. As from a great distance, he observed his body drive the car up to the house and stop it, turn off the engine.

He sat, numb and exhausted, feeling the darkness creep up with the silence and settle down outside the car, waiting for him to turn off the lights, to get out and walk towards the door.

"What have you been doing since I saw you last?" *This, this is what I have done, this house and its contents; without you I have done this, and grown older. And it holds me, soft and implacable, and I cannot fight. Not even a whimper. Was it for this?*

Her white arms lifting in supplication, like drowning Helle, so heavy she could scarcely lift them from the dark water. The light barred her flanks, gold and dark honey: that was from another age. Oh, then his life had filled him tight, then he was full and hard under a thin pliant skin!

The warmth seeped out of the car, and he grew cold as he sat staring ahead, knowing that he must go in and that the longer he sat the harder it would be to explain why he had sat there so long. He looked down at himself, lifting a hand and turning it over, and the pity rose in him in a warm flood. *Jesus God, I'm fat!* The pity of it, oh the pity of it, of his soft body and his deadened spirit, and the endurance of his life that had taken the place of both joy and suffering. He felt round, soft tears seeping out of his eyes as he tried to fix them on the house he could not clearly see.

This is what I have done. Was it for this? Oh the pity – her white arms – the leafy smell of whisky on her breath as she swayed towards him, never quite touching him, in a hundred bars, the undefiled. *Oh, what have I done? And what can I do in the little time that is left to me? For now, suddenly, it is nearer to the end than the beginning; and I am empty.*

One

1960

It was the first Christmas after he had left home. He was twenty-four years old, and his freedom had come late, hard-won from his mother who had opposed him with bitter and experienced energy. There had been times before when he had wanted to leave, but his requests had been half-hearted, for he knew his mother's strength. That summer, however, he had known he would get out.

For one thing, the way had been paved by his elder sister, Douglass, who had by persuasion and trickery got as far as London where she was pursuing her career of photography. Hamil, too, had career to plead, for it was that summer that he had got his appointment to the SNO, the first step up his own ladder. Then, of course, there was the sex business: not that Mother knew about that – God forbid! – but his secret and half-guilty knowledge gave him a strength worth pitting against hers.

It amounted to quite a lot when he considered it, which he did often, for with his Catholic background – his mother was from the west coast – each separate copulation was a point scored against the Church and repression. He kept score – he was still able to keep score – and swelled with each deed into more and more of a match for his mother, who, he was sure, no longer had sex with his father. It was only at this age that he had begun to consider his parents as sexual beings, and then with shakings of the head.

It had been a very sexual year for him in every way, from his enjoyment of the freedom of the single-end in Fountainbridge which he shared with a like-minded horn player from the same orchestra, to his newly sensual approach to his music. The trumpet was something you played with your whole self, and music was his whole passion. You couldn't separate the two, he had discovered.

So when Christmas came after only four months of freedom, he was in two minds whether to turn up on Christmas Eve as was expected of him. Everyone had to be there on Christmas Eve. Douglass was coming home with her new fiancé, an American financier called Morton Halliwell, and Frances, five years younger than Hamil, was bringing her English friend from university. That would please Mother. Like many a Morningside dame before her, she regarded all things English as the apogee of elegance – which was why, of course, she kept such a "traditional" Christmas, with the Tree and all the trimmings. Olivia Porsen, Frances's friend, had the kind of accent Mother would have given her back teeth for, and there was bound to be an extra show put on for her.

So Hamil would be chancing his arm to go missing. Yet he considered it, wondering whether it would emphasise his freedom more to go or to stay away. In the end he decided only not to decide. He was a great believer in putting things off so that they could decide themselves. To the old saying "a letter unopened for a week doesn't need answering" he added an extension of his own: "a letter unopened for a month doesn't need opening". Let Fate decide, and then Fate was responsible. As a Catholic, he knew very well the value of passing responsibility to a higher authority.

In the event Fate decided to compromise. She – he definitely saw Fate as female – kept Hamil occupied until six thirty on Christmas Eve, and then left him stranded, all his friends, including his flatmate, having gone away for the two days. There was neither drink nor comfort to be had at his own address, and it was beginning to snow. He shrugged, thrust his hands into his pockets, and trudged off towards Morningside.

Mother opened the door herself, flinging it wide and standing with her arms a little from her sides and her head back. All her gestures were designed for larger audiences than her Fate had secured to her.

"Ah," she said. "Hamil." The "ah", he realised, had been begun before she saw who it was, and quivered with magnificent welcome, whereas his name had been spoken on a downward cadence of disappointment. He waited a moment while her cold eyes flickered over him and her mind clicked through the procedure of selecting which aspect she would hang her disapproval on. "You have missed the Tree," she said at last. Hamil smiled disarmingly.

"What a charming dress, Mother," he said, kissing the air beside one cheek as he passed her. It was a flowing thing of emerald-green chiffon with great hanging sleeves, a dress which would be as much too big for any occasion as his mother herself was. She was deflected.

"You have no bag with you," she observed. "Surely you are not intending to spend the whole of Christmas dressed like that?"

"Like this?" He looked down at himself as if surprised. He was wearing tight, low-waisted trousers, a woollen shirt and a leather jacket, all he needed in those hot-blooded days, all he wanted to show off his newly discovered sexuality.

"It is hardly suitable," she said severely.

"Oh, no one will be looking at me," he said cheerfully, "invisible as I'll be against your splendour."

"Can you not see, Hamil, that it is not fitting? It is selfish and thoughtless of you to take so little heed of your appearance. An insult to our guests and to me. What can you be thinking of? Can you imagine how it would look if I were to arrive at one of your concerts dressed as you are dressed?"

Hamil began to smile. "Sensational, I should think," he said. Had he ever been afraid of this woman? He wondered at himself.

She seemed to him all at once rather ridiculous than terrible. He could not be bothered, he found, to frame excuses for her.

"It is not a joke, Hamil," she said sternly. She had no sense of humour, none. Hamil smiled on at her, placidly.

She tilted her head, puzzled at his reaction. "I think you are not yourself."

"Am I not, Mother? Who am I, then?"

"I think," she said, controlling her ferocity, "that you are drunk. I know you believe drinking and smoking becomes your worldly image, but you will find in the end that it coarsens both your body and your perceptions. Great art does not come out of a bottle."

"Don't worry; it's only a phase of adolescence. I expect I'll grow out of it," he said. He felt, by now, quite light-headed.

"You are twenty-four years old. And you are not amusing." Her reptilian eyes flickered over him, and she withdrew, inexplicably as a snake.

He followed her into the drawing room. It was a lovely room, spacious and beautifully proportioned in that special manner of the Georgian houses of Edinburgh; elegantly bare with its white walls and dark-blue carpeting, the heavy velvet curtains drawn against the black-and-white night. The tree stood, softly shining, in the corner beside the grand piano. A fire blazed in the grate under the Adam fireplace; bowls of hothouse freesias stood in the alcoves before gilded books; pools of muted light were spread by the three lamps, carefully positioned to illuminate the room to its best advantage. There was a sense of theatre about it, and an artful beauty he valued more at that time than nature. Despite his childhood imprisonment, he could not help a joy of homecoming to this room, if to nothing else.

His father and his older brother Fergus sat like mirror images on either side of the chessboard, both tall, lean, very dark – they even wore the same style of spectacles. Fergus took his off for a moment to look across at Hamil and smile a greeting; his father, whose move it was, remained fixed on the board.

Ewan, the youngest of the family, sat playing the piano quietly – improvising, by the sound of it – and did not look up as Hamil entered. Douglass and her fiancé sat side by side on the long chesterfield where they had presumably been talking to Mother.

"No Frances?" Hamil asked.

"She's gone to collect her friend," Douglass answered. "How are you, Hamil?"

"I'm fine. I don't need to ask how you are – you look marvellous."

"This is Morton," she said, as if it were a reply. "Morton, my brother Hamil. The middle one of the family. The handsome one."

Hamil smiled ruefully at the old, teasing handle, and shook hands with Halliwell. He was stocky, greying. It was not immediately apparent why Douglass had wanted him.

He stood up to shake hands with Hamil, and smiled in anxious affability.

"How do you do? I'm pleased to meet you. I've heard all about you from Douglass, and I've been looking forward to meeting you very much."

"I doubt if you could have heard *all* about Hamil," Ewan said from the piano, proving he was not wholly absorbed in his playing, "or you probably wouldn't have come."

"I beg your pardon?" Halliwell said, politely puzzled. Hamil glanced at Douglass, expecting her to defend her man against Ewan's licensed rudeness, but she turned her head away with a kind of bleak pride. She would not justify her family to her man or vice versa. Never complain, never explain – that was Douglass.

"Granted," was all Ewan said, smiling smugly.

"I see you haven't learnt any manners in the last few months," Hamil said crushingly, but Ewan was uncrushable from long habit.

"I've been too busy learning more important things."

Hamil sat down beside the guest and made himself pleasant,

while Mrs Strathearn sat on the other side of Douglass and annexed her attention. There seemed to be little to learn from Halliwell, who seemed mostly made up of politeness. His obsessive courtesy made him seem almost boyish, though that was at odds with his appearance. He called their father "sir", though Mr Strathearn, with his black hair untouched by grey, looked at a glance the younger of the two.

Hamil wondered a little at Douglass's refusal to bail her fiancé out. She seemed to have brought him home in defiance and refused to cling to him in public, dropping him on the hearth rug and walking away as a dog casually, proudly, brings home a trophy. *He stands alone, as I do,* her attitude seemed to say.

Hamil was interested in this new quality of hers. He had always been closer to Douglass than the others. She was the eldest of the family, forced early into a position of responsibility towards the younger children, and she had developed a firmness and authority which had gradually hardened her.

Their mother, while full of ambition for Douglass, with all her forwardness and beauty, had had no time for affection or for the streak of tenderness she saw in her daughter but neither understood nor admired. Douglass, rebuffed, had soon learnt not to offer advances; had grown a carapace that repelled all borders. Now, in response to romance arriving so late, she had developed, it seemed to Hamil, a kind of rough, crooning quality, like a creature unaccustomed to love being gentle with something small and helpless.

It was a thing Hamil would have liked to know more about, and while he exchanged platitudes with Halliwell he watched Douglass closely. But she was too adept at camouflage to be seen against the background of the family Christmas, and only this hoarse tenderness towards her lover told him anything.

"I understand you're a musician too?" Halliwell was saying.

"Too?" Hamil said vaguely. "Oh, you mean, as well as Ewan?"

"Not nearly as well as me," Ewan said quickly. "I am in a different class altogether."

"We all learnt piano and one other instrument," Hamil said, ignoring Ewan. "But I'm the only one who plays professionally. Ewan, of course, is studying composition—"

"I am the genius of the family," Ewan interrupted. "The others merely have a small, commonplace talent."

Since childhood Hamil, like the rest of the family, had allowed Ewan to be rude and bumptious, a sort of tax levied on lesser mortals to be paid to his differentness, his supposed excellence; but after four months away he had forgotten how irritating he could be.

"I'm sorry if he seems a bit loud at times," Hamil apologised to Halliwell. "He's rather excitable. The artistic temperament, you know."

Ewan picked up the sarcasm in Hamil's voice and played a loud discord in protest. Their mother lifted a hand and said, "Don't do that, dear," without interrupting her flow. Halliwell, meanwhile, had missed the sarcasm and had accepted Ewan's temperament as another fact in the Strathearn Guide Book.

Hamil went on, "We tend to spoil him, I'm afraid."

"Please don't apologise," Halliwell said earnestly. "I can understand just exactly how you feel, how proud you must be of him. Douglass has told me about some of his achievements, and, believe me, I'm more honoured than I can say to be connected with someone who is going to be one of this century's great names."

Hamil closed his mouth. He couldn't believe that anyone could say something like that with a straight face. He searched Halliwell's in vain for a gleam of satire.

"Your whole family is wonderfully talented," Halliwell went on. "I believe your mother used to be an opera singer, and your younger sister is studying fine art at university?"

There seemed no point in revealing that his mother had never been an opera singer. It was something Hamil had found out by accident, and it went against a fine family tradition. Mother had always *wanted* to be an opera singer, and the wanting and the regret had grown so strong that they had at last planted this fable, which blossomed and developed into a fine mass of circumstantial detail. Hamil had always meant to expose her eventually, but it seemed now that she could do him no more harm, and it wasn't worth it.

As for Frances, Hamil wondered if this man knew what "fine art" meant, or if he were imparting some strange and exotic meaning to it; but he could hardly ask. He said, belatedly, "Yes, that's right."

Their eyes travelled to Fergus, conspicuously absent from the parade of artistic talents, but Halliwell's politeness did not falter.

"I guess Fergus takes after your father. And of course, the law demands no small ability. It's a thorny thicket."

"That's true," Hamil said. "Anyway, someone has to keep the family business going."

This was hard work. When would Mother offer anyone a drink? Perhaps not until Frances and her friend arrived. Was it possible to slip out somehow to the nearest bar? Under cover of their arrival, perhaps. Old Halliwell would probably like to come, but he was stuck where he was for the duration, poor bastard.

Douglass addressed a remark to her fiancé, and Hamil took the opportunity of escaping to the piano. Under guise of listening to Ewan's playing, he looked out of the window. The snow was beginning to lie now, and he felt the old excitement of the first settling snow of the winter: the childhood sensation that a new and different world was being created under one's very eyes.

There were two girls down there, scraping up the first meagre settlings and snowballing each other. Automatically he registered their age and shape – both accessible to him – and then one of them looked up, saw him, and began waving wildly.

It was Frances, of course. The other, turning now to see what was happening, must be the friend, Olivia. The friend turned back and said something to Frances, who listened, nodded and then beckoned to him. He stared, uncomprehending.

Frances gestured more and more frantically, making some wild dumb-show that absolutely failed to communicate her mind – and wasn't that just Frances all over? Then the friend jerked her thumb away down the street and made the unmistakable lifting movement of the wrist.

Hamil grinned suddenly. *Oh excellent young judge! A very Daniel,* he thought. He nodded, did a thumbs-up, and eased back from the window.

Ewan was staring at him with naked curiosity. Curses. He would have to be let in on the secret, or he would very likely give Hamil away. A few words of explanation.

"I'll come too."

"Not right away. If we both walk out together, it'll look too obvious."

"You must wait for me, then." His eyes narrowed in threat. "You'd *better* wait for me!"

"All right, but for God's sake don't draw attention to yourself."

Mother didn't even look up as Hamil left the room.

Outside the snow muffled his footsteps so that he felt as if he'd gone deaf. Frances bounced round him delightedly like a dog.

"Darling Hamil! Hooray, hooray. This is Olivia. Olivia, my brother Hamil. The handsome one."

The friend's face looked up at him from the frame of a furry hood, smiling.

"You hardly needed to tell me that." The voice was very English, cool and warm together, with a politeness that neither derided nor challenged. She offered her hand – very English again – and when he gave his she held on to it for a moment. She wore no gloves, but her hand was warm, and sexuality seemed to flow through it. Her politeness, her very Englishness, aroused him.

"We have to wait for Ewan," Hamil said, for something to say. The friend detached herself.

"Isn't the snow delicious?" she said. "I never really get used to it."

"We had enough of it last year," Frances said.

"Last year was a lifetime ago," Olivia said.

"This is your second year," Hamil remembered. And then, "We've met before."

She smiled. "Met is hardly the word for it. We passed you in the street once."

"Olivia and I are getting a flat together," Frances broke in, with an air of being unable to contain the great news any longer.

"How on earth did you get Mother to agree?" Hamil asked.

"Olivia persuaded her. It's a lovely flat, Hamil, absolutely *divine*" – an Olivia-word, Hamil inferred at once – "in Thistle Street."

"Good God! You can't possibly afford it. How much is it?"

"Ten pounds a week," she said importantly. "Mother's seen it, and she says it's worth it. And since she approves, Father's paying the rent and half the food bills."

What Mother could see in the situation to warrant the expenditure wasn't immediately obvious to Hamil. "That must have been some kind of persuasion."

"My whole grant only comes to ten pounds a week," Olivia said drily, "so you see my actions aren't entirely altruistic."

Hamil looked at her with interest. She seemed much older than Frances, even leaving aside the sexuality. He couldn't very well ask how old, though.

"Did you come to university straight from school?" he asked. It didn't sound as subtle as it had done inside his head.

She smiled mockingly. "Oh no. I came to Edinburgh to forget."

"Forget what?"

A shrug. "I've forgotten."

He was too busy fancying her to laugh at the joke. Her eyes

looked into his head. "Opacity is not one of your qualities," she remarked.

Frances looked at her with adoration, and at Hamil. "Isn't she marvellous?" She hugged Olivia's arm.

"I expect it's being English that does it," Hamil said mockingly.

"You've been to England?" Olivia asked.

"Yes; to London."

"Oh, London." Her voice was a downward curve of amusement. "You shouldn't equate London and England. They aren't at all the same thing."

"Here's Ewan . . . Come on, we're waiting!" Frances called, jumping restlessly from adoration of Olivia to chastening of her little brother. "We might freeze to death waiting for you."

"Then he could put the scene into his next symphony – the snow falling, the poor shivering wretches—"

Ewan interrupted Olivia sharply. "I keep telling you I don't write programme music." He sounded annoyed and contemptuous.

"You're such a musical snob," Hamil said genially. "You'll never write great music until you learn to be inclusive rather than exclusive."

"You'll never write great music at all, so you can just shut up," Ewan told him, and taking Frances's arm he ran her ahead down the street.

Olivia fell in beside Hamil."Why do you let him get away with it?" she asked. "Is he so much better than you?"

"Ewan's on a different level from the rest of us," Hamil tried to explain. "He creates. I only reproduce music."

"It seems to me to be a very large 'only'," she said.

He shook his head. "All the family create, except me: Frances paints and draws, Douglass photographs. Even Fergus – interpreting the law is a creative thing. But anyone can learn to play a musical instrument."

"Not quite anyone," she objected.

He shrugged it away. "I've often tried to compose. Technically, of course, I'm well able for it, but I don't seem to have any original ideas. Other people always seem to me to say what I want to say better than I could."

"And it's your mother that's told you this? That you aren't important because you don't create?"

"It's true." He was surprised that she so unerringly fingered his mother as the culprit. Either she had had more contact with his family than he had thought, or she was unusually perspicacious.

After a while she said, "You shouldn't denigrate yourself. Yours is an extraordinary talent, to understand other people's art to the extent of being able to explain it. Most people understand very little, and could never pass it on. You must have a great sympathy."

Her face turned up to him was as clear and impenetrable as quartz; and because it had for him only a small vocabulary as yet, it seemed the more significant, and utterly truthful.

"Do you think so?" he said, shy of accepting the compliment.

"Without people like you," she said, "people like me would be deaf, and dumb, and blind."

They reached the door of the hotel and she broke off abruptly. He followed her in, his skin tingling from the shock of the heat after the cold.

"Same again?" he asked her. Olivia had come up to the bar with him for the second round.

She grimaced."I don't think I can drink any more of that beer. Sheep dip. Could I have a whisky? I'm sorry."

"What for?"

She waved a hand, cancelling it. "I forgot – you're not a student. One always apologises for wanting anything more than a half of heavy."

"Expense no object with me," Hamil said gravely. "I think I'll join you in a short. I'd like to get good and drunk before I go back to face Mother."

She raised an eyebrow. "You? I don't believe it. You'd dare anything."

"Do you know me from observation, or by repute?"

"A little of both, perhaps. Mostly observation."

"And what do you observe?"

"You don't really want to know," she said seriously.

"Don't I? Well, perhaps not – unless it's nice to hear." He looked at her steadily, seeing at this close range that she was not as young as Frances, was nearer to his age. What had she done; where had she been?

"What did you do before you came to university?" he asked abruptly.

She smiled without taking her eyes off him, as if she had read his mental processes. He was to learn this social trick himself, but it was then still very effective.

"Nothing. Nothing happened to me before I came to Edinburgh. I came to start a new life here, as a person completely without weight."

"Weightless? Is that how you feel?"

"Not – no, I mean as a word carries weight. Without significance."

"You are not insignificant," he told her, daringly.

She nodded as if in answer to something else. "Not opaque; not honest, exactly; but brave, your own man. Selfish, but responsible: an odd combination."

He felt himself grow warm. "I said I didn't want to hear," he protested.

They couldn't go on staring at each other like this; it was getting too obvious. He wanted to touch her. Her forearm rested on the bar inches from his hand. It was smoothly plump, like a young rabbit. "I want to talk to you," he said. She nodded again, waiting. He closed his hand over her arm, and she didn't flinch or move away.

"That's very honest," she said.

The barman came to them at last, and he removed his hand.

"Two halves of heavy, please." The barman turned away. "What do you want, Olivia?"

"Scotch, please."

"Anything with it?"

"Oh no: a chap at university told me that it was practically a capital offence up here to add anything to whisky."

He liked her light, cool voice, dry in contrast to the voices around her. "So it is, but what I meant was – well, how would you like to learn the quickest way to get drunk?"

"The authentic Scottish quickest way?"

"Absolutely." The barman came back with the beer and a raised eyebrow. "Two Dewars, please, and two wee heavies." He turned back to Olivia. "You drink them turn and turn about."

"What's a—?"

"Wee heavy? Strong ale. I don't know what you'd call it. Comes in a little bottle – very rich and dense."

"Like barley wine?" she hazarded.

"I don't know. What's barley wine?"

She looked at him and raised her hand in amused resignation. "Never mind. We'll get gloriously drunk, and to hell with the consequences." She added, as if to herself, "It can't hurt, just for once."

"What a time you've been," Ewan said when they rejoined him and Frances. "What's this you're drinking, Olivia?"

"Just like a greedy child," Hamil said, "always looking to see what's on everyone else's plate." He was only half joking.

Ewan raised his eyes to Hamil in pretended shock. "You're not plying Olivia with strong liquors, are you? Trying to get her drunk so you can have your evil way with her? Olivia, come and sit here beside me, away from his influence. I warn you not to touch this stuff he's got you – it's deadly."

"Hamil drinks it and lives," Olivia said, seating herself obediently. Hamil sat opposite her, telling himself that it was better to be able to see her face than to be sitting where he could touch her. "Besides, I'm young and strong. I'll survive. We have a gift for survival."

"Who's we?" Hamil asked, but Ewan's next remark overrode him.

"Hamil drinks it all right – that's what's wrong. I wouldn't hold him up as an example of health and beauty."

"What are you talking about, Ewan?" Frances said good-naturedly. "You know Hamil has half of Edinburgh at his feet."

"That's precisely the point," Ewan said, fixing Hamil with a blackmailer's eye.

Hamil tried not to be moved. "Stop havering," he said, trying to sound indifferent. Would he never learn to keep his brother from getting under his skin?

"What point?" Frances asked.

"He's already got into trouble over drinking too much, and the drinking goes with the girls."

"Why don't you keep your nose out of other people's private affairs?" Hamil said angrily.

Ewan smiled on. "Not so private any more, when a lot of people think you'd play better if you spent more time practising and less time in bed – one way or another."

Who? Who thought so? No – Ewan's bluffing, trying to get my goat. I won't be baited. But—

"Hamil is a very good musician," Olivia broke in, using the authority of her English accent to make herself heard.

"How would you know? You've never heard him play," Ewan retorted rudely.

Olivia looked at him coolly, and her voice took on an extra layer of politeness as she contradicted him. "I have often heard him play."

"Have you? Have you really?" Frances asked. Olivia nodded. "I didn't know you were musical."

"I'm not musical. I can't play any instrument – I can't even read music. But I love to listen to it and I've often been to concerts and heard Hamil play." She looked at him. "You are a fine musician. Ewan is getting carried away by his own rhetoric."

It was a kind way of putting it, but it had the effect of squashing Ewan. Hamil felt a flush of gratitude running under his skin to augment the desire he already felt. He lifted his glass to her and drank, and said, "Here's tae us."

Frances and Ewan finished the toast between them.

"Wha's like us?"

"Gae few—"

"An' they're a' deid."

Olivia laughed delightedly. "What is it? Say it again!" So they taught her. It seemed like a rite of passage, making her part of them, taking her into the family. He remembered it afterwards, with mixed feelings.

Outside again, the snow surprised them, for they had all forgotten it while they drank. Hamil knew he was drunk, and the only thing sad about that was that it meant he didn't know if Olivia was too. She seemed just the same, except that her cheeks were pink. She and Frances ran about in the snow like children, their voices echoing flatly on the dead air.

"Look up," she called, staring upwards. "See how it rushes madly down. Like a devil's dance. There should be some music like that."

Frances was turning round and round on the spot, her head tilted back, trying to catch snowflakes in her mouth, until she grew dizzy and sat down abruptly. She giggled. She had no head for drink, and Hamil wondered if there would be trouble over her state when they got home. If they ever got home.

"I'll write you some music," Ewan was saying.

"Will you?" Olivia said as if humouring a child, as if she didn't believe it.

"Yes, I will. I'll write you a whole symphony!"

Hamil looked at his brother's sallow face, with a red spot high on each cheek, and his fierce eyes. "He means it, you know," he warned Olivia.

She grew grave and looked from one of them to the other.

Frances got to her feet and put her arm round her friend. "Of course he means it. He'll write you the music, and I'll illustrate it – I'll paint this scene for you." She made a rather drunken sweep of the arm, but her sincerity was apparent. "And Hamil can play it for you. We'll make it a real family effort."

They surrounded Olivia and, though they were pressing gifts on her, she smiled uncertainly at the ring of faces almost as if threatened.

Then she put her arms round Frances and hugged her. "You've a nice family, Frances. It must be nice to have a family."

Frances expanded in the warmth of her love. She smiled at her friend, wanting to give her everything. Hamil understood the feeling – wasn't that what this scene was all about? "Poor Olivia – you never had any family, did you? You can share mine, of course you can. You'll be her brother, won't you, Hamil?"

For a fraction of a second Hamil and Olivia exchanged a glance, and then she began to laugh, saving him the trouble of replying.

"I'll make do with you, Frances, my old china. You mustn't ask people embarrassing questions."

"My old *what*?" Frances looked puzzled, and the moment passed, and Hamil fell in behind them and listened to the rambling explanation of cockney rhyming slang that followed as they walked home.

Two

June 1961

The door was a large, white-painted, panelled affair, probably original to the building, with a brass handle and a brass lion's-head knocker which probably weren't. He knocked with the ring through the lion's nose and waited.

Under the knocker was affixed a large white card with their names written on it in Frances's own special art-school lettering and bold black ink. "Olivia and Frances", it said, reminding Hamil, with an inward smile, of the cards on the doors of Glasgow prostitutes. He wondered if their mother had seen it.

He knocked again and still received no answer, so he put his head against the door to listen. Very faintly, he heard music. Having regard, then, to the thickness of the door, they probably couldn't hear above the music. He was about to knock again, but the brass door handle, on which he was leaning, gave a little under his hand, and, trying it, he found it opened the door. Trusting of them, he thought, and walked in.

The house – or "flat", as Olivia called it in her English way – was on the first floor of a close in Thistle Street, the best floor to be on, where the ceilings were high and the cornices and moulding handsome. It was large and airy and sparsely furnished. The floors were parqueted and the walls distempered white, and what furniture there was was dark, heavy and antique.

He had glanced in at three rooms without discovering them, so he stood in the middle of the hall and called. "In here!" came the faint reply. He followed the voice and opened the door, to find himself in the bathroom.

By contrast to the rest of the house, the bathroom was like some tropical jungle – hot, steamy, dark and noisy. The walls were papered with a dark-green, leafy pattern, the floor was carpeted in dark green, and there was a green blind over the window. Standing in pots on the floor were some tall, vaguely tropical-looking plants with large glossy leaves, and their number was multiplied into a forest by their reflections, through the steam, in several long mirrors about the room. It was the most exciting bathroom he had ever seen – a thousand miles away from the sternly humourless, white porcelain laboratory at home.

In the bath, with her hair skewered on top of her head and a dew-beaded tumbler of dark liquid in her hand, was Olivia. In an armchair beside the bath, engaged in de-stoning peaches and, presumably, attending to the record player from which came the *Rococo Variations* at top volume, was Frances. They both smiled at him, and Olivia greeted him with a queenly wave of the hand.

"Fetch yourself a glass from the kitchen. There's plenty left."

He complied, finding time to swallow down his embarrassment while he was out of the room. It wasn't as if you could *see* anything, he told himself angrily, through all those bubbles, but his middle-class upbringing was shocked – and shockingly aroused. He had a stern struggle with himself before he returned.

At Olivia's direction, Frances gravely filled his glass from a jug at her feet.

"What is it?" he asked, for want of something to say.

"Black Velvet," Frances told him, watching his face, and then, seeing that he didn't know, as she hadn't until Olivia had initiated her, "It's a mixture of stout and champagne. We often drink it," she added proudly.

She had taken the stone out of another peach and given half to

Olivia, and now shyly offered Hamil the other half. He took it, bemused, and then tried the drink. It was cold and surprisingly sour, but invigorating.

"Peaches," he said. "Champagne. How on earth can you afford these things?"

Olivia bit into the fruit, neatly catching the juice from her chin with a swipe of her tongue. "There's a simply marvellous shop in Nicolson Street that has English cheeses and German sausage and real bread and a very comprehensive wine counter," she said. "So life is bearable after all."

He wanted to say something rude, feeling that she was putting on some kind of an act to impress his sister, but he was still not at ease in her bathroom, so he repeated instead,"But how can you afford them? Champagne must cost the earth, and *peaches—*?"

"I opened an account," she said simply.

"We pay for it at the beginning of term," Frances said quickly. "When our grants come in."

"How did you open an account when you're only students?" he asked, bemused.

Olivia laughed. "Gall," she said. "If you order enough of everything they never think of asking you for cash. It's the great advantage of the fine old Edinburgh class system. But you look shocked, poor Hamil – why?"

"I'm not shocked," he said, hastily rearranging his features. "I'm just wondering how you pay for it all."

"Frances told you," she said, a trifle impatiently.

"But then you have to run up another bill through the term because you've no money left. And then what? Who bails you out?"

"Don't be so parochial, Hamil," Frances said. He saw her looking from him to her friend, anxious that neither should show up badly, or say the wrong thing. "We're not intending to bilk the tradesmen. Olivia gets a job in the summer – and I will too, of course," she added hastily, though Hamil knew that she would be unlikely to get their mother's permission for a summer job. "And we'll pay for everything out of our wages. Having an account isn't *wrong*. Mother has an account at Jenners."

Hamil paused on the brink of reply because he saw the amusement glinting in Olivia's dark eyes, though she was making an appearance of studying her glass while they argued with each other. At length he addressed her instead, and in what he hoped was a worldly, easy tone.

"You're very devious, you know. You really ought to have been called Livia."

Frances caught the reference. "After the Roman empress? Oh, but wasn't she frightfully cruel?"

"Manipulative, rather," said Hamil.

"You're way behind us, big brother," came Ewan's voice, closely followed by his head round the door. "I've been calling her 'Livia' for weeks. Is that more blackers? Yum yum. Wait till I get a glass."

"Blackers?" Hamil wondered at the familiarity.

Ewan's head was withdrawn, to return moments later. He came into the bathroom with every appearance of familiar ease and held out his glass to Frances to fill. "Right to the top, Fanny," he said, and smacked his lips ostentatiously, like a schoolboy. "You've a head start on me, since you didn't tell me you were making. There I was, sweating away—"

"You here too?" Hamil found his voice belatedly.

"Working," Ewan said defensively. "In the other room. I thought I heard your voice."

"How can you work without a piano?" Hamil asked. The record switched itself off with a loud click, and in the silence that followed he heard one of the bath taps dripping, and the pale ticking of the foam in the bath.

"He thinks he's Beethoven," Olivia said with amused tolerance. "He sits there with a piece of paper and a 2B pencil and swears he can hear every note. He's going to turn into one of those horribly dull people who take a score to concerts and read it ostentatiously all through the most swooning performance."

Ewan had reddened slightly, and he spoke defensively. "As it happens, I'm only going over some stuff I've already finished; and, as it happens, I *can* hear it in my head. Any musician could. Hamil will tell you."

Hamil was so surprised and touched at Ewan's appealing to him – Ewan, the genius, appealing to Hamil, the hack – that he nodded and murmured, "That's right," before even considering that Olivia was only teasing the boy. His suspicion was immediately confirmed.

"Don't be so touchy; I was only joking," she said. "And now, since the music's stopped, and the water's cooling, and Ewan's guzzled the last of the booze, I think I'll get out, if you three wouldn't mind withdrawing. I must get ready to go out. But don't go right away. You can come with me."

"Where to?" Hamil asked. He saw that Frances, too, had looked round at the question, so she didn't know either.

"To the Botanical Gardens," she said, and her voice implied, "Of coursc," though she didn't say it.

They walked there through the back streets, which Olivia traversed with every appearance of familiarity, and Hamil dredged up from the back of his mind the memory that she had lived in this quarter, in lodgings, when she first came to the university. He had only ever once been to the Gardens, on a school trip when he was twelve or thirteen. Ewan and Frances, he guessed, had never been there at all. Perhaps it always took a stranger to know a city. Years later he was to remember that, when he took Olivia through the back streets of London by ways she had not known.

Olivia appeared to know the attendant on the gate, for they passed in without paying. She at once ran out ahead of them on to the first lawn and held out her arms, like a eurythmics student being a tree. More acting? he wondered, and frowned in faint disapproval. It was too like Mother's gestures. But her purpose was immediately seen to be simpler. A small grey shape ran down from the nearest tree and bolted across the grass to her, closely followed by another.

"Squirrels," Frances said, enchanted. "Look, Hamil, how tame they are!"

"Yes," he said. The first squirrel had run straight up Olivia's body to her shoulder without a pause, and the sight had given him a curious pang.

They had continued to follow her all this time, and now the second squirrel saw them, paused in the grass at Olivia's feet, and then bolted back to the tree. The squirrel on her shoulder ran too, but paused half-way between her and the tree and looked back over its shoulder, freezing with one forepaw lifted and its plumed tail spread behind.

"They've got used to me," Olivia said apologetically. "They're very tame when they know there's something in it for them."

She put her hand into the pocket of her dress and held something out, making encouraging noises. At that the squirrel turned and ran in short bursts, covering the last stretch in a sprint, and received with the confidence of familiarity what Olivia was holding out to him.

"What are you feeding him?" Hamil asked.

"Peanuts," she said. "I buy them in Woolworths. No accounts there, sadly – it's cash only. They say no good deed goes unpunished. See the other one?" It was approaching cautiously from the tree. "That's the female – this one's mate. The females are always shyer."

Frances and Ewan clamoured for peanuts to try for themselves, and she handed them over. The male took them boldly.

"Just like a hoover," Frances said, pleased. "One whoosh and it's gone. Oh, the poor female, she's getting nothing!"

"She'll come in a minute. Greed will overcome fear," Olivia said.

When the nuts were gone, the squirrels deserted them at once. Olivia caught Hamil's eye. "So much for friendship," she said.

"You can't expect altruism from a member of a different species," he said. "That was symbiosis."

And she grinned. "Didn't I tell you so at the very beginning? But we do things so much better, don't we? At least we make pretence that we don't do it for the peanuts. Let's go to the tropical house."

In the sultry, green-smelling damp they strolled, separated from Frances and Ewan, who had walked down another aisle, out of sight and earshot behind the tropical creepers.

"This is where I got my rubber plants," Olivia said. So Hamil learnt the name of the vegetation in her bathroom.

"Of course," he said gravely. "Bought them?"

She turned to smile at him. "Given them," she said. "I got talking to the keeper."

"How people seem to love giving you things!" He remembered the scene outside the hotel on Christmas Eve.

"People like giving anyone things," she countered. "You only have to show an interest. People like to have the things they love valued."

"You are a schemer," he said.

She looked slightly hurt. "Not at all. I *am* interested. And if it gives people pleasure to give me presents, why should I hurt their feelings by refusing?"

"You could offer to pay for them," he said, and then realised at once how silly that was. "No, scrub that – of course you couldn't. I suppose I'm just jealous. No one ever wants to give me things."

"Except themselves," she said. He met her eyes and the painful feeling reasserted itself. "That's your talent. You should be glad that you have such an unmistakable persona. I seem to be all things to all people. Whatever a person most wants in a companion, they imagine I'm it. I fulfil their dreams without having any reality of my own."

"Isn't that your talent?" Hamil asked.

"How can it be a talent to be so featureless everyone mistakes you for someone else?" she asked. "I want to be loved for what I am, not for someone else's projected dream."

"I should have thought all love was rather like wishful thinking," Hamil said cautiously.

"Do you think so?" she asked at once. She had stopped and was standing under a trailing plant that reached down and balanced its lowest leaves on her shoulder. He was reminded of the squirrels. "Yes, I suppose you're right. Oh well." She turned and walked on, the trailer lingering regretfully on her shoulder until the last possible minute. Her voice came back to him cheerfully. "Perhaps people recognise me by my featurelessness. Perhaps characterlessness *is* my character." She hummed a few bars from the *Rococo Variations* and reached the end of the walk. "I think I'd like to go to the pictures. Where are the other two?"

They took a bus back and went to the cinema in Lothian Road. Hamil noticed with amusement how Ewan manoeuvred himself so that he was sitting next to Olivia and how Frances helped him to do so. Hamil himself took the seat on her other side, which was what he wanted though perhaps not what he ought to have had, for he found it very difficult to concentrate on the film. The whole of the side of his body nearest her seemed extra sensitive, as if she were radiating.

His mind was full of images of her body – in the bath, of course, and standing on the green feeding the squirrels, and in the greenhouse decorated with ivy; and other images he hadn't known he had stored, from other times. Her body . . . He felt rather ashamed of himself, as if she might read his thoughts and be hurt. Poor Olivia – it was not how she wanted to be wanted. Were they all so selfish? They all wanted her, but for different things. Frances saw her as the leader of the expedition, an adventurer into unknown territories, who would ultimately lead her, Frances, to freedom. Hamil simply wanted to go to bed with her. And Ewan – he paused, not sure about Ewan. What strange fancies lurked in Ewan's mind regarding Olivia he could not yet be sure.

Olivia stirred in her seat beside Hamil and part of her leg came into contact with his. With any other female, at any other time, he would have done something – pressed back with his leg or inched nearer or taken her hand – but he forced himself to stay still, as if he had not noticed. Perhaps she had done it deliberately, but he could not take the chance – she was already too precious. And they would have to discuss the film afterwards, so he'd better try and watch it.

He left them as soon as they came out of the cinema, although it was still a little too early for the concert. The pubs were open, so when he got near to the hall he dropped into the bar the musicians used, and found his mother there, sitting at a corner table with the ease and confidence of a *habituée*.

"Hello, Mother," he said uncordially. He knew she would smile at him, and that was worse than her criticism. He felt that all the others in the orchestra laughed at him over his mother.

"Hello, Hamil. You're early, aren't you?"

"So are you, unfortunately," he said.

She frowned through her smile. "You might remember your manners and at least pretend to be glad to see me. I am, after all, still your mother," she said lightly, trying to convey a reprimand for his ears only.

"I wish *you'd* remember it," Hamil said *sotto voce*, and looked around ostentatiously. "Which one is it this time?"

She seemed surprised at his boldness, and he was a little surprised himself. It was, at least, uncalled for, since he already knew she was having an affair with the lead bass player, a giant of a red-headed Scot called Nicol Webster. With his gentle speech, quiet, courtly manners, and his huge, broad frame, Webster was in direct contrast to Hamil's father, which was why, he supposed, his mother had chosen him. It made it no better that he liked Webster very much, and that Webster was evidently embarrassed by the situation.

Hamil stared at his mother with bitterness. It had been bad enough when she had had affairs with barristers, magistrates, and the Chief Constable; bad when it was operatic tenors and visiting soloists, as if in exchanging the legal for the musical world she was taking her spite against him instead of against his father; but now she had actually started on his own orchestra, and on musicians at his own level. There was at least something grand in debauching with a famous conductor, but if she was now reduced to trawling for ordinary orchestral hacks – that was doubly humiliating.

Rarely had he hated her so much as at this moment, but there was no time for either of them to say anything, for Nick Webster had seen him and had come across to ask him, with a charming hesitant stutter which was entirely unstudied, what he wanted to drink. In his presence, mother and son reverted to the distant politeness they maintained with each other most of the time.

"And what have you been doing all day?" Hamil's mother asked him brightly. She lavished a brilliant smile on Webster as he handed the drinks, but turned back to Hamil so that he knew she meant to be answered.

He took a draw at his pint before answering.

"I've been with Ewan and Frances," he said, picking his words carefully. For some reason he didn't want to mention Olivia to his mother. Why? Did he think she would detect in his tone of voice something of what he felt about Frances's flatmate? What did he feel? This was no time to be soul-searching. His mother sipped at her drink – gin and something, probably – and licked her upper lip in that animal way she had which Hamil hated. He could imagine her saying "yum yum", as Ewan had earlier, in a mock-greedy voice. She probably *thought* "yum yum" when she watched Nick undress – there was so much of him. But it was very necessary not to think of his mother doing that with Nick

Webster. Hamil discovered he was shaking with emotion, and tried hard to control himself.

"That's nice," she said vaguely. "Where did you go?"

"To the Botanical Gardens," he said shortly. She nodded.

"I thought Ewan was going over to see Olivia this morning. That's what he told me, anyway."

"So you knew about that?" Hamil said before he could think what he was saying.

"About what?"

"That Ewan was visiting Olivia," he muttered, angry with himself.

"Oh, was that where you met him?" Mrs Strathearn was enlightened. "Why didn't you say?" She looked sharply at her middle son, the handsome one, to whom everything came so easily. What was he up to?

"I didn't want you spoiling his fun," Hamil said dishonestly.

"But why should I object to his visiting Olivia?" she said, sweetly. Hamil's fists balled at his side, and he carefully undid them and picked up his drink. "No, I'm very happy with that little arrangement. Olivia's a charming girl. Charming."

So that was it. Ewan was to be given Olivia, as if she were simply one more random present, something he coveted and must therefore have. Did she really think Olivia charming? Probably. Olivia was all things to all people, and had a tendency to fulfil the roles handed to her. She was, even to herself, the blank canvas on which each person painted his own image. Mother evidently wanted to think of Olivia as a younger version of herself.

"She isn't charming at all," he said abruptly. "Did you know she has an account at the most expensive shop in Edinburgh, and encourages Frances to run up enormous debts?"

Mrs Strathearn smiled this away. "You mustn't exaggerate, Hamil," she said. "Olivia, of course, has immaculate taste, and naturally finds it hard to live on a tiny grant. Besides, it's good economic sense to live on credit, as I'm sure your father would tell you if you were to ask him. You must try not to be so censorious and small-minded. I can't think where you get it from. I was never like that – I always did and said just what I wanted. Honesty is a very valuable trait. I see the same kind of honesty in Olivia. I think she must have a very large soul."

There was so much confused and confusing material in this that Hamil could not answer. He drained his pint in an angry movement and then wished he hadn't, for it made his head swim, and he hadn't eaten yet. He thought of Olivia drinking Black Velvet in the bath. Of course, Ewan had passed back the stories of how she lived – probably Frances had unwittingly been pumped too – and his mother was now recasting herself in the attractive role of the bright young thing as described by her two youngest children. Ewan was to have Olivia – or perhaps, his mind suggested with a halting sickness, it was that Olivia, otherwise Gillian Strathearn, was to have Ewan. He was old enough to understand that his mother might be afraid of ageing and pining after her lost youth, but not old enough to pity her for it.

"I don't want to b-be a bore," Nick broke in at that point, "but I think we ought to b-be getting dressed soon."

"Good gracious, is that the time?" Mrs Strathearn chirped, glancing with something of a flourish at her watch. Hamil followed the direction of her eyes. It was a new one, a narrow gold watch with a guard chain. He glanced irresistibly at Nick, who blushed, though he might have done that anyway. "Yes, you two had better go on," she said. "I'll meet you here afterwards, shall I?"

This was evidently meant for Nick, and not for Hamil, but the big man hung his head in embarrassment and seemed to expect Hamil to answer for him.

"You won't see me," he said shortly. "I've an early start tomorrow."

"No, darling, I didn't mean you," Mrs Strathearn said, and her hand came out and took hold of Nick's arm caressingly.

Hamil glared at it, that small, white, plump hand with the long, well-kept nails. It was very much a lady's hand, but it grabbed at what it wanted like a greedy child. And she always got what she wanted, of course.

He plunged out of the bar, leaving Nick to say to her in private whatever needed saying. He didn't want to hear.

Inevitably, after the concert, he went back to the girls' flat. The alternatives were to go home or to go out drinking alone, since his mother would be sitting in the orchestra's pub waiting for Webster. (As, on occasions, girls had waited for him. But sex was forgivable in oneself, or in the young.) He bought a half-bottle of whisky on the way, to make sure of his welcome, before remembering that only Olivia liked whisky.

But as it happened she was alone there. The door was still on the latch, and Hamil found Olivia sitting cross-legged on the floor in the sitting room, listening to Tchaikovsky's E minor symphony. She didn't move as he appeared in the doorway, waiting for the last few bars to end, rocking slightly on her crossed ankles.

When the record stopped she looked up at him. "Shall I put on the other side?" she asked.

"If you like," he said politely, "But a little lower, perhaps."

"Then I won't put it on. You don't really want to hear it, and it isn't background music."

She got up in one fluid movement and went away from him across the room to turn off the machine. He felt a little annoyed with her for presuming to tell *him* about music, she a mere listener, while he was a professional; but he badly wanted not to quarrel, so he said instead, "You've had your hair cut." It had been a sleek page-boy bob; now it was short and layered like a marigold.

"I had to," she said, as if that were obvious. Her necessities were as obscure as they were apparently random.

"You don't ask why I'm here," he said next.

She stood where she had stopped and considered this.

"Did you want me to ask?" she said eventually. "Is there some particular reason?"

"No – but I didn't think you'd be expecting me."

"You have to be somewhere," she said. "And Frances is your sister."

"Yes, Frances," he said, as if he'd forgotten her.

"She's out. With something called Bill."

"You disapprove?" he asked, amused.

"I've never met him," she said flatly, "so I can't very well approve, can I?"

She had a way of short-circuiting him, and he found himself stopped again. He remembered the whisky and tried again.

"I brought you this."

"Oh, good. That's marvellous. Let's drink it now, shall we?" She came across to him quickly and took the bottle, looking up into his face and smiling, and it was at that moment that he saw she had been crying. It startled and worried him, for he could not connect her with unhappiness, but this did not seem to be the moment for asking.

"Shall I make it up into a drink?" she asked. "I know it's supposed to be sacrilege, but if I drink it neat I may get drunk, and I'd like to remember everything about this evening."

The implications of this were so perilous that his mouth dried and he could neither answer nor ask her what she had meant.

She took his silence as acquiescence. "Sit down, take your shoes off, make yourself comfortable while I go and mix the drinks. Make yourself at home. I know that sounds like a lower middle-class cliché, but I mean it – I want to revel in you being here in my house, sitting in my chair, being comfortable in my sitting room."

He smiled a query and she clutched the bottle in a childlike gesture of excitement. "I never quite get used to you," she said, and left him to think about that one.

The room was softly lit with lamps, pleasantly warm, and very comfortable. He was winding down from the concert and had she been long in the kitchen he might have fallen asleep. As it was, by the time she returned with a tall jug and two glasses, he was absolutely relaxed, his hands in his lap and his head back.

She paused at the door and looked at him, as if admiring the view, and then without speaking she poured him a glass of dark, marmalade-coloured liquid that rattled with ice-cubes, handed it to him, and then sat again, cross-legged, on the carpet in front of him.

He tasted the drink. It was excellent, and he raised an eyebrow in enquiry at her.

"It's called Suspension. It's a cocktail. A barman invented it specially for me."

"Why?" he found the energy to ask.

"Oh, I suppose because I took an interest. People like giving me things."

"You said that before," he said, and then wished he hadn't because it shut her up. "What's in it?" he asked to make her speak, though he had guessed.

"Whisky, pure orange juice, and ginger wine. It was the barman in—" She broke off abruptly as if catching herself on the brink of an indiscretion.

He stirred, curiously. "Yes? The barman where?"

She looked away from him, shrugging to herself. "The Braid Hills Hotel."

He frowned. "That's a bit out of your usual way, isn't it?" It was very proper, very expensive, and pretty remote into the bargain – a long bus ride for a person without a car. And the sort of place where a woman dropping in on her own would be looked at very much askance. "What were you doing there?"

"I was with your father and Fergus. And some business associates," she said in a flat voice that invited no questions.

He found nothing to say about it. He could not imagine why his father and elder brother should have taken Olivia there, but on the other hand he could think of no reason why they shouldn't. It seemed at once an absolutely extraordinary and quite unremarkable piece of information. And it effectively short-circuited him again.

In the silence that followed they both sipped and looked in other directions. When she had topped up their glasses Olivia reached out and touched his foot.

"Men's ankles are so terribly unexpected," she said without looking up. "They look so frail."

He looked down on her close-petalled head and had a strong desire to touch it, the hair looked so thick and springy. "My mother calls you charming," he said.

She looked up at that. "Does she? I don't think I like that. It's a kind of lurking insult."

"No-o," he said, thinking about it. "I don't think she means it as an insult. I think she's rather afraid of you. Because she can't quite account for you. She doesn't know what you're going to do or say next."

She seemed amused. "And do you?"

"No – but it doesn't worry me."

As he said it, it sounded false, and Olivia nodded and said, "Ah," as if she had discovered something she was going to keep to herself. Then, "Was she there tonight? At the concert?"

He nodded.

"But your father never goes, does he? Why is that? He seems so proud of you—"

"Does he?" Hamil broke in, surprised. "I thought everyone regarded me as the family failure." He was at once ashamed of revealing such bitterness to her, and went on quickly, "But that isn't why he doesn't come. It's because he can't stand the idea of patronising my mother's lovers."

Worse and worse; now he had betrayed his mother and his hatred of her. But Olivia only nodded, and suddenly he relaxed. He could do no greater harm. Perhaps, in any case, Olivia already knew, as she seemed to know so much. He said, "I don't object to her taking lovers – that's her business. But it's when she does it so blatantly – it hurts my father, it hurts his standing, and it makes me a laughing-stock. She had to choose my orchestra, of all things. She could have had the entire male population of Edinburgh, but she had to choose—"

Olivia nodded sympathetically. "Yes," she mused. "It's strange how evil an ordinary thing can become when there's ill will on both sides. She half does it to spite you all, and you resent it because of other, old wounds. And yet intrinsically, what has she done? No more than you yourself do."

"I'm not married."

"Perhaps even what your father does."

"Father never would." She said nothing, and he went on angrily, "You condone it? You take her side?"

She looked up at him, her face moulded in light and shade as if he might reshape it with his hands: not unfinished, yet not finite, not fixed. *This is mine*, he felt, *to make and mould*, even while she was moulding him.

"I only observe," she said. "I see that you care very badly about what your mother does, but your father – I don't believe he cares, now. A man content in himself is unassailable."

"I don't understand," he said, forcing himself to be honest when he would rather seem omniscient and superior.

"It's just this," she said. "What use is sex to you? What do you get out of it? I rather suspect you get as little out of it at the moment as your mother does, and that, if you got more, you wouldn't care much what she did."

He had asked for it, but he could not quite take it. It left him with no feet on the ground at all, and he had to scramble for a foothold. "Don't you think you're rather young to talk about sex like that – unless of course you're speaking from the depths of experience?"

Well, it was said, and there was no unsaying it; but he saw in her face not acceptance of the rebuke, but disappointment, and he felt the opposite of what he had wanted to achieve. Instead of feeling bigger, he felt smaller. He was suspended in mid-air with no recourse but to hit out, smash, shout – or change the subject.

Or – or else . . .

Hamil dropped out of his chair on to his knees, grabbed her clumsily, and kissed her. Her lip caught on his eye tooth and he felt her flinch and try to work it clear. He eased the pressure, but held her with no room for escape and kissed her thoroughly, expertly.

It was meant to silence her, no more than that; but it was his undoing, for what ever else he did not take seriously, he could never make love with half his attention. He quickly forgot why he was doing this, and as she relaxed against him after the first recoil and then put her arms round him, he reached a point from which it was harder to go back than to go forward.

She withdrew her mouth from his, but he did not release her. She said against his ear, "It's very unfair of you to do this."

"Why unfair?" he asked, having forgotten how it began.

"Because you make me want you. You would feel properly offended if I did that to you with no intention of carrying it through."

"Who says I've no intention of carrying it through?" he asked, kissing her ear and cheek with practised skill.

"You *had* no intention," she said. "Have you changed your mind?"

He twisted her round and laid her down on the carpet. His movements were all commercial, the unthinking, ritual movements of the standard seductive procedure he used on all girls in the same kind of situation. But he hung over her and met her eyes. Few people ever looked straight into one's eyes, in his experience, and it forced one really to look at the other person and consider.

His self-regard slithered out of him, leaving in its place a devouring kind of wanting that made him feel hollow and shaky and hot. He licked his lips, almost frightened by the force of wanting her. He thought she would speak again, but there was nothing to say. As if movement pained him, he lowered himself against her and sought blindly for her mouth.

The stages of the act that usually took so little time seemed almost unbearably protracted, as if they were moving in slow motion. Yet they had no time to undress, and in its merely mechanical details it was as little and sordid as any hasty screw he had ever had. So why was it different? His body felt swollen and hypersensitive, as if there was no covering to his nerve endings. He seemed to touch her when the surfaces of their skin were still inches apart; all his senses were taut, relaying messages to his brain about things he would not normally have noticed.

And she was so real to him, so absolutely *there*, that he was not doing things to her, alone and remote as in every sexual act he remembered, but was seeking her out, and finding her everywhere he reached, coming into her with a sense of relief as in coming home. Sharing with her, being with her, sensing her pleasure through his, reaching out with her for something he could not obtain alone. She moved, touching him, speaking to him, so that even though his eyes were closed the dark was peopled with her. He was not aware of what she said, or that he replied, only that speech was a part of their coition, another kind of communication. And when the climax surprised him, bursting out of no particular crescendo, he tried not to have it, felt it taking him away from her. What before had been his only object became an unbearable disappointment.

Her arms were around him as he convulsed despairingly against her, and she spoke consolingly, even while he was struggling to say, "I'm sorry."

"It's all right, it's all right," she said.

"I'm sorry. I tried not to. Oh darling—"

"I'm sorry too. I wanted it to go on for ever. Greedy," she rebuked herself lightly, but something in the quality of her voice made him look at her, and he saw she was crying again. An unbearable tenderness engulfed him like a second ejaculation.

"Darling. Livia. Don't cry. I'm sorry. It will be better next time," he said, stroking the tears away from her eyes, frantic at their being replaced as quickly as he cleared them.

"Next time—" she said on a funny, broken note. "Hamil, I love you."

Even through the welter of new emotions, he felt the old, cold fear at those words. He stiffened a little, and began to withdraw, and at once she relaxed her hold on him and said in a comfortable voice, "It's all right – first times are never much good."

A statement which both of them, in the circumstances, knew to be as untrue as it was dishonest. It silenced them both for a moment. Then she said, "We mustn't be caught like this. Frances will be coming home. We'd better get up."

He felt in control again, now that she was awkward and embarrassed by her own clumsiness. He stopped her moving and said smoothly, "Will there be a next time, Livia?"

She pushed him back a little so that she could look at him, and removed a sweaty thread of hair from his forehead before answering.

"I should think there would have to be, don't you?" she said. "I don't see how either of us could leave things as they are."

"I'm glad you feel like that. I was afraid—"

"Don't be afraid," she interrupted. "Fear will kill it."

"I didn't mean that," he said, embarrassed.

"I know what you meant," she said; then in a different, lighter tone, "Next time we must arrange matters better. This floor is too hard for pleasure."

He laughed and eased himself up. "You're right. Hell on the knees," he said. "Pour me some more of that drink while I go and tidy up."

When he came back she was sitting as she had been before with two full glasses, and everything was back to normal. She had made it possible for them to survive the experience, he thought, taking the glass she held out to him. There is a kind of social code, after all, even in sexual encounters.

"Hamil," she said, and the use of his name startled him. "Would you mind keeping this a secret?"

"I hadn't intended to tell anyone about it," he said, "but on the other hand—"

"If it isn't a secret, Frances will get to know, and Ewan. And if they know, your mother will know."

"I don't see why that matters," he said, puzzled. "She must guess that I—"

"I don't want your mother to know," she said fiercely, and he saw she was afraid. "She changes things."

Slowly he relinquished the newly realised idea of wiping his mother's eye. Livia was right, of course.

"All right," he said. "But we will – I mean, go on with it?"

She smiled, relaxing suddenly like someone in a drama class told to register relief. "I meant what I said," she confirmed. It wasn't until much later, on his way home, that he realised what that remark referred to.

Three

August 1961

"Excuse me," Hamil said to his host, "there's a back over there I know."

"The bare one? Lucky fellow."

A bare back above a black satin evening dress, and a golden close-petalled head. He eased his way through the crush and tapped her on the shoulder.

"I thought I knew that back," he said. "You'll have to come along of me to the police station."

"Why's that, Mr Plod?"

"Because I can't remember the way." They smiled at each other with satisfaction, a ritual completed. "I never know where I'll meet you next. What are you doing here?"

"I came with the head of the School of Music – one of my drinking buddies."

"I didn't know he drank," Hamil said, looking round for him.

"My dear! Why else would he be known as the Don with the Luminous Nose? You can usually find us in the upstairs bar in Deac's, if you're interested."

"Of course. The only place in Edinburgh where they sell draught Guinness."

"But what are you doing here? The wilds of Colinton can't see you very often."

"One of the chaps in the orchestra is going out with our host's sister."

"Sally? Who isn't?"

"Now, Livia, don't be catty. It doesn't suit you."

Her face straightened. "Sorry. Carried away by the sparkling repartee. Not a bad party, is it?"

"It's improving," he said, smiling down at her.

"Darling, you do say pretty things. You must practise them all the weeks I don't see you."

"It isn't weeks—" he began, but she cut in smoothly.

"You mean it doesn't seem like weeks to you?"

"Of course, but you know it isn't my fault."

"You could come round."

"I could, but I can never see you alone. Frances is always there, and Ewan too, as like as not. I see you all over Edinburgh, but never alone."

She frowned. "I know. It's difficult." The crowd pushed her at him, and she folded her arms across her front, her right hand shielding her glass of whisky. She caught his downward glance and said with a wry smile, "This is the kind of dress that men look down."

"I was looking at your glass, actually. How come you always manage to get a decent drink in these days of cheap plonk?"

"Simple, my dear Holmes. I bring my own. Come into the bedroom with me and I'll give you some."

"How can I refuse an invitation like that?"

He followed her as she wormed her way through the crowd, greeting and cracking jokes with almost everyone they passed. Her acquaintance seemed enormous, and one or two of them raised an eyebrow at Hamil as if wondering who he was.

They inched past a closely embracing couple in the passage and entered the bedroom where the coats were piled on the bed.

"No one here, thank heaven," Olivia said. Hamil closed the door behind him, and she turned at the sound, smiled, and put herself into his arms to be kissed.

Some minutes later she broke away from him, panting.

"Whoa! That's enough of that," she said.

"I haven't even started."

"Not here, Hamil. It's too frustrating. Have some whisky." She rummaged for her coat, took a half-bottle out of the pocket and passed it to him.

"Thanks."

"You sound disgruntled," she said when she took the bottle back from him.

"I've told you why. Every time I see you, there's someone else with you. I don't see why you need to know everyone in the entire city, and see them all several times a day."

"Gross exaggeration," she said calmly, sitting on the edge of the bed and filling her glass. "Most of the people I know are university people, or contacts of theirs—"

"Like the head of music? And Prof Roberts?"

"Why not? He teaches Frances Latin – of course I'm friendly with him."

"You don't need to be that friendly. Frances says you're the only student who goes into the staff club."

"Frances says it as a boast," she said, "and it is not true." She tilted her head enquiringly. "Why so sore? You're a busy man too. And not all the people you're seen about with are male or over thirty."

He felt himself redden. "Who's been telling you tales? I don't—"

"Hush, hush. I'm only teasing."

"It's just that sometimes I wonder if—" He stopped, too embarrassed to finish. He had been feeling increasingly that their one sexual adventure meant more to him than to her. She was on his mind all the time with a mixture of desire and doubt, for it seemed that she made no effort to see him alone, and yet when he did see her she treated him with great affection and a kind of teasing intimacy, as at present. Any act, if repeated often enough, achieves a kind of legitimacy – the reason, perhaps, for multiple murders. Equally an act left in isolation draws from that very isolation more and more uncomfortable associations. Hamil had at first been eager to repeat the encounter with Livia; then anxious; finally, he was almost desperate.

"Well?" she prompted, and when he didn't go on, she said, "As a matter of fact, a large proportion of my free time is spent with your family in one way or another."

"Free time? I thought all your time was free now?"

"No; I've got a job, a part-time job." She grinned engagingly. "I'm a City Guide."

"What's that?"

"I collect a party of sightseers from the Castle Esplanade and walk down the Royal Mile with them, explaining and pointing out as I go along. I take them as far as Holyrood House and then collect another party to bring back. I have a badge from the City Tourist Office to show I'm authentic, and the tourists give me large tips for my trouble."

It was impossible to be surly with her. "And how do you know what to tell them?"

"There's an official book we're supposed to mug up. What I can't remember, I make up."

"Olivia!"

"The Americans are best – they tip enormously. And I put on a variety of different accents. The Morningside one comes off best. I can do your mother to a tee."

"You'll end up in prison," he warned her.

"They believe anything I tell them, the darlings," she laughed. "They're so obedient and credulous, as if they're doing it for their health."

"You're wicked." He shook his head. "And how much of your time does that take up?"

"Oh, it varies. You have got a one-track mind, Hamil."

"You said you'd been spending your time with my family."

"All right," she said crossly, "I'll give you a sample. On Monday I went skiing on the artificial slope with Frances and Ewan and some other people from college. On Tuesday I walked round the golf course in the Braid Hills with Fergus while he played. On Wednesday—"

"All right, you needn't go on. I believe you."

"On Wednesday I had tea in Fullers in Princes Street with your mother—"

"With Mother?"

Olivia smiled at him. "And Frances. She was keeping her eye on us – she thinks we live riotous lives in that flat. We were very subdued and proper, I can tell you."

"You lead a charmed life. You and Fanny in that flat "

"It *is* wonderful," she agreed. "For Frances, I mean. I just wish she'd go out on her own a bit more. But still—"

"What are you doing tomorrow?" he asked suddenly. "To-morrow afternoon?"

"Riding, out at Polton," she said promptly. "And after that, I don't know. I'll probably drop in at the Jolly Carters on my way back."

Stumped again, he thought. He took the bottle from her as she held it out and took a mouthful.

She watched his face, wondering about his mental processes, and said gently, "How are you getting home? Have you transport?"

"My feet," he said wryly.

"It's a long walk home from here, especially if you detour over the hills to see the moon. I think we'd better start right away, don't you?"

He looked at her, opened his mouth to say, "Didn't you come with someone?" and then shut it again and took the hand she held out. Gift horses, et cetera.

Despite what she had said, the following afternoon found him with time on his hands, wandering along Thistle Street. There was no answer at the flat, so Frances was evidently out too, and on an impulse he decided to drop in at his father's office, which was in the same street, to see him. The impulse was probably connected, subconsciously, with his unsatisfied curiosity about Olivia. A case of putting all his enigmas in one basket, perhaps. He walked back along the street, pondering over the coincidence of Livia's finding a flat so close to his father's office, until he entered at the high door into the dim, furniture-polished, cloistral atmosphere of an Edinburgh lawyer's office.

Miss Rattray, his father's secretary, whom Fergus had, perhaps inevitably, rechristened Ratbane, was for once not in her wonted position. Normally she was inseparable from her heavy desk, which was placed centrally in the office opposite the door, a physical and psychological barrier to the stairs to the upper floor. Anyone wanting to get at Mr Strathearn had naturally to get past Miss Rattray. She was not an unhandsome woman, but she wore half-glasses for distance viewing, and there was something menacing in the way she put back her head to look at each new arrival. It was almost as if she were baying.

But this once she had deserted her post – though there was a half-finished letter in the typewriter, so she hadn't gone far. To the lavatory, perhaps. Hamil imagined Fergus's astonishment at discovering that Ratbane was as much a servant to nature as the rest of them. Bad show, anyway – anyone could walk in and visit his father unannounced, as he now proposed to do.

He mounted the stairs to the first floor, to the single, white-panelled door. No brass lion's head, he noticed – otherwise the door was identical to Olivia's. In fact, they occupied exactly the same position in their relative houses, the only difference being that the girls' door was in a close. All the dwellings were built this way along the street, alternately a public close and a private house.

He tapped perfunctorily and went in. The room was enormous and sparsely furnished, nothing at all happening for the first two-thirds of it. His father's desk stood in front of the defunct fireplace at the far end. His father was there behind his desk, and in the chair in front of the desk was Olivia.

The three of them were still for a moment, like characters in a tableau. His father was held in the act of rising from his chair – his hands were in front of him on the desk to push himself up, and there was something weary about the gesture. His shoulders were stooped, his head forward as if his neck were tired of carrying it. He looked tense, but not alert – a man in the prime of responsibilities.

Olivia, on the other hand, was relaxed in the chair, almost sprawled. She was dressed to go riding, and with her yellow, polled head and her riding breeches she looked very English, formally casual as only the English can look. She looked very, absurdly like herself. Both she and his father were looking at him as if they had been startled in the middle of a conversation. Hamil took a step forward to apologise for butting in, and in that moment, when movement flowed back into the room and released them all, Olivia looked quickly across at Mr Strathearn.

Why did it seem to Hamil so significant? Because the look was flung between them so quickly? Was that necessarily suspicious? Yet there was something in their expressions, something Hamil might have expected between two adults who knew each other very well, not between Olivia and her best friend's father. Was it a look of entreaty or of warning? Did she seek or give reassurance? The swiftly exchanged glance, that afterwards he even thought he might have imagined, seemed to establish Olivia and his father on such terms of intimacy that for the first moment it was almost visible to Hamil in the sunlit, dusty room.

"Ah, Hamil," his father said, as if he had been expected, and the two of them had simply been whiling away the time until he arrived. "There you are."

"Hullo," he said awkwardly. "I was just passing, so I thought I'd – just . . ." He let it trail away, realising how absurd it sounded. "I thought you'd gone horse-riding," he said instead to Olivia.

"Horse-riding – how funny that sounds," she replied. Her voice was warm and friendly, just as it always was.

"What should I say?" he asked, a little huffily. She ought to sound different, after last night.

"Not a matter of 'should' – it's just that a person who rides never says 'horse-riding', only just 'riding'."

"It's a thing that isn't much done here," Mr Strathearn said. "It's considered rather superior and English, so only the very rich do it."

"But I thought you were very rich," Olivia said, turning to him and laughing. There was something caressing about the quality of her teasing of Mr Strathearn – something that echoed the protectiveness that Hamil felt towards him. "After all, you have a big house and you play golf and have more than one suit. You're middle-class" – she pronounced it with the Scottish broad "a" – "and in England riding is very much a middle-class hobby."

"All my children were taught golf, and music, but we couldn't run to horses. We treat animals differently here – if they do not work, we have no use for them." Mr Strathearn smiled at Olivia for a moment, and then turned his head to draw Hamil into the circle. "We don't even keep a dog, do we?"

Hamil was annoyed. He felt all this was a smokescreen. He wanted to ask what Olivia was doing here, but he hadn't the right. He wanted one of them to ask him what *he* was doing here, though he hadn't an answer. He muttered something ungracefully, and saw Livia's damned telegraphic eyebrow flicker.

"Your Cerberus isn't at her post," he said abruptly, "so I thought I'd come and warn you that you might be invaded."

"I already have been, twice," said his father, and his voice was kinder, less ambivalent than usual. "It does not follow that the invasions must be unwelcome. I am honoured to be the focus of attention of the younger, busier set – or did you arrange to meet here?"

Olivia looked at him, but didn't answer. Hamil said, "I just dropped in as I was passing. I thought Livia had gone riding."

"I was going," she said, and didn't offer any explanation for her change of plan. "Did you go up to the flat?"

Hamil nodded. "Where's Frances?" It was the nearest he could get to the nagging question.

"In George Square gardens. Reading Roman history. A last-minute cramming session in the hopes of fooling her humanities tutor – some hopes! He's as easy to fool as a radar screen. Listen" – she straightened abruptly in her chair – "shall I scram? I expect you two want to be private."

She looked at Hamil as she said it, and he, not particularly wanting to be alone with his father – wanting much more, though he couldn't say it, to be alone with her – hesitated. Then he looked at his father, began a preparatory-to-going, negative sort of movement, and read in the parental eyes some inexplicable hostility, a gleam both cold and malicious, like a crocodile's.

"It seems not," his father answered her question, ineffably polite. "Well, Hamil? Have we anything to say that Olivia might not hear? I'm sure she is a party by now to all the family's secrets, both pleasant and unpleasant. Isn't that so, my dear?"

Suddenly the atmosphere had changed. Something had been said – something had been breached, letting the cold air in. But what? She had offered to leave Hamil and his father alone. What was wrong with that? She had altered the pairing, that was all. It had been Olivia and his father on one side, Hamil alone on the other; she had stepped away from Mr Strathearn, conversationally speaking, and now, somehow, it was Hamil and Olivia together, his father alone. How had that happened? And why did it matter? Good God – the thought suddenly occurred to him – was his father jealous? And if so, of what?

Mr Strathearn had turned that faintly malicious glint on to Olivia. She looked back steadily, thoughtfully. "What was that fable, about the king who couldn't keep a secret? So he was told to go and stick his head into a river." She stood up. The glance she gave his father was no girl's look. It was, perhaps, admonitory. "I'm that kind of river, except that I don't have any rushes to give the game away. Just a deep, slow old river. The big hole down which people throw their sandwich papers."

"Your imagery, as always, tends to diminish the significance of what you say," remarked Mr Strathearn. He had risen too, and they were staring at each other across the barrier of the desk like two dogs barely restrained from going for each other.

"It is intended to," she said.

"I did not suggest the tendency was involuntary."

"Well, what do you want me to say?" she said impatiently. "If you want a crisis, you surely don't have to reach far for one. I didn't ask for all these confidences."

"You accepted them. I'm afraid responsibility can't be shrugged off. It's an old man of the sea." Hamil saw how stooped his father's shoulders were, how lined his face. "And please don't threaten me. You forget I'm a lawyer."

Hamil could see that this last was an attempt to placate her, an attempt at a joke, but Livia had reached the end of some tether of her own.

"If you provoke me, what can you expect? I won't be poked with sticks all the time."

"Olivia—"

"Oh—" She made a flat gesture with her hand. "I'm sorry. Forget it. I'd better go now – are you coming, Hamil?"

They were both looking at him, and he had suddenly to recover his expression of bemused concentration and look unconcerned.

"Did you want to see me about something?" his father asked him politely.

"Nothing that can't wait," Hamil said hastily. "I'd better be going, too."

"Well, do drop in, any time you're passing," said his father politely, and Hamil could not for the life of him tell if it was a sarcasm or not.

Outside, Olivia turned toward the flat without a glance at Hamil, and he hesitated, not knowing if he was meant to accompany her or not. She gave him a brief, uninterested glance. "Come on," she said impatiently, like a distracted mother to a child. He felt stupid, tagging along beside her after that, but he would have been more stupid to draw attention to himself by standing on his dignity.

She walked quickly, as if to walk off a temper, but when they reached the front door of the flat she stopped and turned to him with a charming smile.

"Will you come in? We could have some tea."

"You sound terribly English," Hamil said. Her eyes held his, and he found his breath shortening as he realised that she meant for them to make love again.

He spent a rapturous, dizzying, exhausting hour with her, and went on his way afterwards like a drunkard. It was only that night, in the privacy of his single bed, that he wondered if she had done it to distract him from the questions he might otherwise have asked. About his father. About her and his father. Questions which she almost certainly would not have answered.

April 1962

Douglass was coming for a weekend visit, because she was pregnant with the first Strathearn grandchild – which was a cause for family celebration – and because her husband was away and pregnancy was making her jittery. He learnt of the first of these reasons from his mother, who demanded his attendance. The second he learnt from Douglass herself during a quiet moment when they were alone together on the evening of her arrival.

Mrs Strathearn and Frances were in the kitchen preparing the next meal. Ewan had gone out to the hotel down the road to buy a bottle of wine and had pressed Olivia into accompanying him, Mr Strathearn was in his study finishing some necessary work, and Fergus had momentarily wandered off on some purpose of his own. Hamil and Douglass were left alone in the drawing room together for a few pleasantly relaxing minutes.

The fire had been lit, for the afternoon was chilly, and it had not yet grown dark enough for the curtains to be drawn and the lights turned on. Douglass reclined in one of the big armchairs, her fair face flushed with the firelight. She looked calm, wonderfully beautiful, and much softened, both in features and expression. Hamil, perching on the arm of the chair opposite her, watched her admiringly as she stared into the fire.

She had always confided in him more than in any other member of the family. Probably she would not have told anyone else of her nervous fears. They remained in a sympathetic silence for a while, until Douglass roused herself sufficiently to study Hamil as he had been studying her. She came to the point in her usual direct way.

"What is there between you and Olivia?"

His reaction was instinctive and defensive.

"Nothing."

"It doesn't look like nothing. You watch her all the time – stare at her. The air crackles with impure thoughts."

Hamil gave up the impossible. "Am I that obvious?" he asked pathetically.

It was scarcely in Douglass to be tactful, and she struggled for a moment with the alien element. "Mother's noticed."

"Christ," Hamil said softly. "What did she say?"

"It isn't what she *says*." She paused. "I think she expects her to marry Ewan."

"Marry!" Hamil said explosively. "What can she be thinking of? Olivia and Ewan? Ewan's only a boy."

"Olivia's fond of him."

"As a boy – as a brother. That's all – I'm sure of it. She doesn't love him."

"Does she love you?" Douglass asked bluntly.

Hamil was forced to think about it.

"No," he said at last, reluctantly. Those golden occasions – what could he read into them? Perhaps the safest way for him and for Olivia was not to read anything into them, to accept them, as one accepts the weather, for an aspect of the time they occupied. "She's fond of all of us, but I think Frances is the one she really loves."

Douglass stirred at this, for love was for her a word with a limited usage, and she could not say as freely as Hamil that one could love a friend.

"And do you love her?" she asked, kindly, for she didn't want him to be unhappy.

"I don't know," he said at last. "I think about her a lot." He wanted to talk about her, but though Douglass was the member of the family to whom he could confide most, he could not talk about sex to her. His upbringing held him back – his sisters would always occupy for him a particular, consecrated place in his life and in his thoughts. "She's a very interesting person," he finished lamely.

"Perhaps." Douglass was cautious. If she had ill opinions, she would guard them until it was clear whether or not Olivia would become one of the family. "Ewan, at any rate, finds her so."

Hamil held his tongue. He had seen from the beginning how Ewan had dogged her footsteps, and how she had borne it patiently, with the patience of an only child. He could not believe there was more to it than that. But women were unaccountable in their decisions to marry, so rarely was there any apparent benefit to them in the transaction.

"Why did you marry Morton, Douglass?" he asked on the train of that thought. Having asked, it was too late to realise how rude the question sounded, but he saw that she had not taken offence. Relaxed and warm in the deep chair, she let her mind wander freely back and investigate the conditions of her courtship.

"Why does anyone ever marry?" she said at last. "For what afterwards seem very inadequate reasons. You don't decide all at once, of course. He says, 'Will you?', and you say yes, because it's the best thing to say at the time, and there's always time to back out before you actually go through with it. And there goes on being time, even to the very point of the wedding, and then it's too late to say no, after all.

"But there's a different kind of time after that. It goes on being all right. Even when it isn't rapturous, it's tolerable, and probably better than the alternatives. And you think, even then, *If I wanted to, I could go*; and so you don't go."

"Is that all?" Hamil asked, appalled. "It sounds so – bleak."

"It isn't, not when it's happening. Perhaps from time to time you think, *Why isn't there more to it? More excitement, more passion, more positive happiness* – as opposed to the mere lack of unhappiness – but then you think, *After all, it wouldn't be any different with anyone else*."

"You surely don't believe that? In that case, you could marry anyone – there'd be no point in choosing any one person rather than any other."

"When it comes right to it, you don't really choose. A person is in the right place at the right time, that's all. How many do you choose between? Not even two, for most people. But even if you had unlimited choice, there's only a limited number of ways to live with a person. You work, you keep house, you eat and sleep. Most of your adult life is spent working, most of the remainder is spent eating and sleeping – repairing the fabric of your life. There are very few moments when it matters significantly who you're living with."

"Then why bother at all?"

"Because those times – the times when it matters – came too often here at home."

"What do you mean?" Hamil was puzzled.

Douglass's face contracted briefly round her reply. "Mother."

"Oh." Flatly. "You minded very much about her?"

"You don't know, Hamil, you still don't know, what she's like. Of all of us, only you were ever free. I don't know why – whether it was something in you, or just chance – but she never got hold of you the way she got hold of the rest of us. That's why she resents you so much – because she can't control you."

"But I *wasn't* free – she *did* control me," Hamil protested. "It's only since I moved out – and then I was only following in your footsteps."

Douglass shook her head. "I know that's how it seems, but even when you lived under her, it didn't really touch you. I always knew you'd get away. You did what you were told, paid lip service, but she never really *had* you, and she knew it. She couldn't get inside you. But me – even in London I couldn't escape. Marriage was the only way I could finally get free of her." She lifted her hand and slowly, slowly clenched her fingers. "Morton's a good man – a *good* man, I mean. He has fine standards. He gives me what I need."

Her speech had flowed, but on reaching this point she found herself suddenly embarrassed, as if she had exposed too much, and she looked away from her brother, and put her flushed cheek in her hand to hide it. Hamil, too, looked away. It seemed such a functional view of life, so comfortless, that he didn't want to take it in. What place had love, or passion, or ambition, or pleasure in such a life? What was the point in living at all, if one lived only to stay alive? It couldn't be right – it must be a partial view. Perhaps it was a woman's view? He grasped at the let-out. She was pregnant, and all pregnant women got depressed, had fancies.

"But you are happy?" he blurted out, after all. "You are happy with him, Dodo?"

She heard the appeal dimly through her own thoughts, the extra appeal of the childhood nickname. Of all the family, Hamil, the handsome one, had been closest to her. She had nursed him as a baby, at a time when she needed something small to love, but before the responsibility for the younger ones' defence had become a burden. Hamil, a charming baby and a delightful young boy, had trotted after her and called her Dodo, and she had dressed him up and taken pride in curling his fine hair and matching the woollens she knitted for him to the blue of his eyes.

And he was young still – not so much in years, but still full of dreams and ideals, high sentiments and plans for the future, loving her, wanting her to be happy, without the maturity to live with the knowledge that those he loved were not always, not even often, happy.

"Yes," she said. "I told you, he's a good man. You must come down to London and stay with us, and get to know him. You'd like him."

And in this, at least, she knew her Hamil. Morton was exactly the kind of man Hamil could like – a man to be admired, but who, nevertheless, constituted no rival.

Later that evening, Ewan played some of his new work on the piano, while Olivia, at his request, turned the pages for him. She could not read music, and he had to tell her when to turn, and it would have been much easier for someone else to turn for him, but it was her he wanted. Hamil watched them from across the room, glowering, feeling the intimacy between them, until he caught his mother's eye upon him and composed his features. Olivia's attitude towards Ewan's attentions seemed to him more than acceptance. Rimmed with light from the standard lamp behind her as she bent over the music, she seemed lovely and remote, out of his reach. Douglass's words had registered in his mind more than he knew.

He saw his mother watching them, read in her satisfaction a better knowledge of the situation than his own. And why not? Ewan, the genius of the family, had passed matriculation at sixteen, had been invited at fourteen to become assistant organist at St Giles Cathedral, had won the Dalhousie Concerto Prize when barely more than twelve. Was it possible to believe that Hamil, a mere orchestral musician, could be preferred above that glittering prize? What had he to go on, but a few passionate encounters, and that uncanny way they had when together of knowing each other's thoughts? He didn't know if that was enough, or even anything at all, and to try to discover the answer would be to risk horrible hurt and humiliation for himself.

His struggle was hard and short. The next time Douglass visited, a month later, Hamil brought to the family dinner a young girl called Irene – a local girl, presentable, passably pretty, with nice manners and a commonplace mind. She was evidently much in love with Hamil, who treated her with a kind of insolent charm.

Though shy, Irene was by no means overawed. Her social manner was the complete answer to the Strathearn family, and her upbringing had provided her with a neutral response to any question that might be put to her. Not understanding them, she did not perceive them to be anything out of the ordinary, and she very soon felt quite at home with them, and they, equally, with her.

After a while it became supposed that they were going steady. Since Hamil did not live at home, and since Mrs Strathearn did not want him to think she was interested in his affairs, no one asked him if he and Irene intended to marry, but they were talked of as a couple. Frances liked Irene, and quietly, shyly, made friends with her, and said nice things about her to Hamil to let him know that she approved of his choice. Hamil noted this with concealed amusement. Let them think what they liked about Irene. It was Olivia he wanted to impress.

He watched her, darkly, for her reactions, and if he saw none, generally invented them afterwards. But it was all very unrewarding. He would never find out what she really thought, for in taking on Irene, he had to forfeit Olivia's confidences. No one spoke of their inmost feelings when Irene was present.

Four

October 1962

From talk of freedom Hamil moved to thoughts of escape. For some, freedom is the ability to establish a chosen identity, as Douglass had done. But for Hamil, as for many escaping prisoners, his principal desire was to establish anonymity; and like many before him, he went to London.

The choice was obvious, logical. Douglass was already there, living near Bond Street, from where she was running an anything-but-anonymous photography business. She had broken through the society barrier which, by its recognition and patronage, divides the passport-and-wedding service from the legitimate art form. In certain circles, a portrait by Douglass Halliwell was as necessary an accoutrement of status as a Lamborghini or a pair of Afghans.

Douglass herself relished the money and fame, was half amused and half frightened by the patronage. The former gave her the freedom to extend her own mastery over her chosen form of expression, for she was a photographer in the sense that Ewan was a musician. The latter she combated with a sturdy independence of soul, a dignified and Scottish superciliousness that made it possible for her to refuse to be lionised, and which, with the perversity of fashion, made her presence at social gatherings all the more sought after.

She was delighted that Hamil was coming down, and offered him all the help he needed. Morton found him a place to live, at his request, in the unfashionable end of Kensington, and Douglass made the flat ready for him by buying a couple of good pictures and stocking the larder and drinks cupboard. For the rest, he fended for himself.

The move was made possible by a vacancy which occurred in one of the London orchestras. Hamil went for an audition without much hope. In the nature of things, since there were so few orchestral trumpet places, competition was always fierce; and he was young to be co-principal of such an eminent orchestra. He knew and had even played with the man he assumed would be favoured. But the random luck sought after by house-hunters blessed him, for the principal of the section was a fellow Scot. He had several acquaintances in common with Hamil, and his patronage was sufficient to tip the balance in Hamil's favour: it was immensely important in a small section for the members to get on together, both personally and musically. So the appointment was his. The escape was accomplished in five weeks.

Everything about his new life delighted him. He had twice – three times as much work, and consequently very nearly three times as much money. The variety of entertainments and the paucity of free time to explore them made London seem like a cornucopia of experience, and it was not until age and disappointment had blunted his sense of wonder that he changed this opinion. His flat was larger and more comfortable than his place in Edinburgh, and he could afford better food and drink on his higher salary.

Most of all, his new job demanded a higher standard of musicianship, was far more exacting and more satisfying. It was the orchestra's boast that every member of it was capable of being a soloist, and they frequently chose concert programmes with the purpose of proving that their boast was also their pride. The average age of the players was remarkably low: Hamil found himself for the first time in the company of keen and able musicians of his own age whose company solaced his starved sociability, and whose ability spurred his ambition and competitiveness.

He began to be very happy.

June 1963

News from home filtered through to him slowly. In London, even people living in the same "village" frequently see nothing of each other from one year to the next, so it was not surprising that he and Douglass, living in villages as far apart as Kensington and Mayfair, had little contact. It was from Douglass, however, that he received the news of the next break-out, by means of a phone call that reached him late at night.

The phone was ringing as he arrived at the front door with Simon Grey, a bassoon player in the orchestra with whom Hamil had become very friendly. They had been drinking after the concert and had decided to bunk down for the night at Hamil's, which was nearer the venue for the next day's early session than Simon's Ealing home.

Fumbling with the key, Hamil let himself in and grabbed the phone, leaving Simon to turn on the lights and close the door.

"Hello! Hello!" he shouted into the mouthpiece in the vague delusion that the caller was moving away in disappointment.

"Don't shout, Hamil. You're awfully late – where were you? Your concert finished at a quarter to ten."

For one horrible moment he had thought it was his mother. Their voices were similar on the telephone. "Having a drink with a friend," he answered. "How do you know when the concert finished?"

"I made it my business to know. I have an interest in your career."

Hamil had tilted the mouthpiece away from him to say to Simon, "My sister. Help yourself to a drink – you know where?"

"You're not alone," Douglass observed. "Is this inconvenient? Shall I ring off?"

"Darling discreet Douglass," Hamil laughed. "It's only Simon. How could I have thought you were Mother?" There was a brief silence, and then Hamil added, "Yes, I am just a wee bit fu' – what the Londoners call Brahms."

"Brahms?"

"Brahms and Liszt – pissed. Simon's teaching me about English beer. It's quite different from heavy. For instance, did you know—"

"Darling," Douglass interrupted. That at least was a Londonism: it was not like her to call anyone "darling". "Not now. I want to go to bed. Listen, what I wanted to tell you was that Frances is coming down."

"Frances?" A moment's thought. "For a holiday?"

"No, for good, or for as long as she can last out."

"That's terrific. Hooray! When is she coming?"

"Tomorrow. Morton's found her a little place, and I'm getting her a job in a gallery just along the road from my studio, so I'll be able to keep a distant eye on her."

"Is she coming alone? What about Livia?"

"Olivia can quite well look after herself," Douglass said sharply.

"You don't like her, do you? Why?" Hamil was curious. There was a short pause.

"I don't know. I can't help it. I suppose I should be grateful to her, since it must have been by her help that Frances has got permission to come. But there's something about that girl that I can't like."

"I think she's all right. She's very good-hearted, and she's very fond of Frances."

"Perhaps that's what I don't like," Douglass said. "Frances could do without being swallowed up any more. Anyway, it's up to her what she makes of this opportunity. I've done what I can."

"And what do you want me to do?" Hamil asked. "I'm sure you didn't just phone to keep me informed."

"How well you know me," Douglass said, without humour. "I

want you to meet her from the train and take her to the flat. I'd go myself, but I've a client at that time, and Morton's going to Brussels first thing tomorrow."

"Well, all right, if I can—"

"Oh, you can all right – I checked on that. She's arriving on the two o'clock train, which gives you plenty of time to get there from your rehearsal."

"All right. King's Cross, I suppose? And what do I do with her?"

"That's up to you – and her. A bite to eat, probably, and then show them the flat – I'll give you the address. I'll probably pop round during the evening to tell Frances about the job."

"Wait a minute – you said show *them* the flat?"

"Olivia will be sharing the flat with Frances," Douglass said. "She can find herself a job without my help."

"But what I want to know is, how on earth did you manage it?" Hamil asked. He and Frances and Olivia and Simon Grey were sitting on the floor in the girls' new flat, sharing a meal from the Chinese take-away during a pause in a mammoth game of mah-jong. The talk had drifted to the wonder of Frances's being here at all.

"Oh, it wasn't me – it was Livia. Sheer magic, wasn't it, Livy? I don't know how you do it."

"Persistence," Olivia said. The change in Frances since she had arrived in London was enormous, and evidently delighted Olivia as much as it did Hamil and Simon Grey. To Hamil, Olivia seemed painfully the same, or perhaps a little more desirable.

"She won't tell me how she got round Mother," Frances complained, "but it was wonderful to watch. First letting me cut my hair, then coming to London—"

"It suits you," Hamil put in.

"Which – the hair or London?"

"Both." He smiled at her in genuine pleasure. "The hair makes you look really pretty, and London makes you sparkle. I like your new clothes, too."

"Livia chose them – she's got marvellous judgement."

"The truth is," Livia broke in, laughing, "I've got a marvellous staff discount, and Frances has got a marvellous figure."

"As flat as a board," Hamil agreed solemnly.

"That's marvellous nowadays."

"You work in a dress shop?" Simon asked, surprise just apparent in his voice.

"Not just any dress shop, but Biba – and not behind the counter," Livia said comfortingly. She too had noted the nuance. "I'm personnel officer."

"I didn't know you were a personnel officer," Hamil said, surprised in his turn. "When did you train for that?"

"I didn't," Olivia said. "The job was vacant, so I applied for it. You don't need training to be in personnel. You just need spoof to get through the interview."

"Livy could get herself a job as a brain surgeon if she wanted," Frances said complacently. "I honestly believe there's nothing she couldn't do."

"Oh, there are one or two things," Olivia said airily, but Hamil saw the shadow that crossed her face briefly.

Perhaps not entirely irrelevantly, he asked, "So Ewan's all on his own at home now – except for Fergus?"

"He doesn't care," Frances said robustly. "He's so thrilled about being taken on by Auerbach that he wouldn't even notice if Mother and Father left. And he's started a symphony, and he thinks it's going to be wonderful, and he says Auerbach thinks so too. At least he thinks his ideas are good, as far as he's got them written down – Auerbach does, I mean—"

"The same thing, of course," Hamil said drily. "Still, I'm very glad for him." It sounded inadequate, as indeed it was. He was very proud of his brother, but it was hard to put into words, for he had so often been accused of, and sometimes even guilty of, jealousy of Ewan's talent, that anything he said was likely to sound ungracious.

Livia looked across at him and, as if she knew his thoughts, said, "He's a law unto himself, and the reasons for which he's happy or unhappy are as much his own as the reasons for which he does things. But at the moment, he's happy."

"And you?" Hamil could not help asking, although it was impossible for her in this company to tell him what he wanted to know, which was, *are you happy to have escaped him*?

"Yes, I'm happy again," she said, which almost told him.

It was necessary to change the subject. "How well you and Frances both use chopsticks," he remarked.

"They've opened a new Chinese restaurant in Nicolson Street, and Livy and I've started to go there quite a lot. A funny little waiter taught us how," Frances said eagerly. The conversation moved on to her new experiences in London, and from there to a more general discussion of the plays that were on at the time, in which Simon and Frances had a lot to say and Hamil and Livia very little. The latter, after a moment, picked up the empty dishes and implements and began to take them into the kitchen, and Hamil jumped up to help her, leaving the other two deep in their discussion.

The kitchen door swung closed behind Hamil, cutting off the sound of the voices in the other room.

"Where shall I put these?"

"Oh – just put them down on the table. I'll clear up later, after you've gone. We'd better fix up something to drink now, hadn't we?"

"OK. The old favourite'd be nice, wouldn't it – Black Velvet?"

It was a deliberate appeal to her nostalgia, but she did not turn.

"Impossible, I'm afraid. Can't maintain those sort of standards down here. Cold lager's the best I can offer, but I think there's some lime for those that like it, and for those that don't—"

"No lime," he finished. She smiled tentatively. "Frances is looking wonderful, isn't she?" he continued.

She smiled more fully at that.

"She's a new person, away from the claustrophobic atmosphere at home. It's what I always wanted for her."

"You're very fond of her, aren't you?"

"Of course," she said, with slight surprise. "I love her dearly."

"And how did Ewan take your departure?" It was a bold question, and she would have been fully justified in snubbing him.

"He didn't notice – it was all done very quickly."

"So you ran away. From him or from Mother?"

"I'm not sure I understand you," she said coolly, but he had gone too far to stop now.

"We all thought that you and Ewan—" Her eyes were hard, and his nerve thinned out. "That is, Mother seemed to think—"

"Could we please not talk about Ewan?" she said impatiently. "He seems to be an obsession with your family. We're in London now; let's forget him for a while, shall we?"

"Did you forget *me* while I was in London and you were up there?"

She turned to face him, leaning against the sink, and smiling at him quizzically. "Unfair question. Did you forget me?"

"Of course not – how could I?"

"It was you who went away."

"I know. But you—"

"I what?"

"You always had so many other pots on the boil."

She laughed. "What a nasty piece of imagery. Too many pots spoil the broth."

"Likewise many hands make light work. Did you remember anything about me, about our – meetings?"

"It's different down here. I never could get used to making love in a goldfish bowl," she answered obliquely. They were smiling at each other now, and he understood that it would be different in London, that she would be his own for as long as their mutual contract was fulfilled.

"I think Frances and Simon are going to get on very well

together," Hamil said as he took the last step across the kitchen to meet her.

September 1963

"I wonder where we'll all be in, say, ten years from now," Olivia said. Hamil glanced down at her. He had been playing in Holland Park, and they were walking back to his flat together. It was almost dark, and Olivia, who was wearing a canary-yellow linen trouser suit over a paler yellow shirt, glowed preternaturally in the fluky light.

"Where do you think?" he said. "I would have thought it depended entirely on where we all wanted to be."

Olivia smiled and shook her head. "Do you think people always do what they want? Or even *ever* do what they want? It doesn't work that way."

"Well, it's their own fault then. I shall do what I want."

"What *do* you want? What are your ambitions?" she asked.

"I don't know yet – that is, not in detail. Of course I know generally, so you can stop smiling in that superior way."

"What, in general, then?"

"Get a principalship – extend my repertoire – go abroad for a time perhaps and play with one of the big orchestras in Europe – then, eventually, I suppose, solo work. End up a revered old man, the ultimate exponent of my instrument, and give master classes."

"And be invited on to *Desert Island Discs*, and receive your knighthood in the Birthday Honours list," Livia finished for him. "Well, I hope you make it."

"Why shouldn't I? Who will stop me?"

"You'd be surprised."

"All right, what about you? What do you want to do?"

"What do I want to do? Or what do I want to be?"

"Are they different? Well, both, I suppose. You don't want to go on working in that shop for the rest of your life, do you? That isn't exactly a career to absorb you one hundred per cent."

"Well, I suppose in my case 'do' and 'be' aren't different things," she said musingly. "In general, I want to be happy, like everyone else."

"That's not much to go on. How about in particular?" Hamil prompted her as they reached the end of the park and turned into Kensington High Street.

"In particular, I want to buy a boat and sail round the world – very slowly."

The idea of doing it slowly seemed extraordinarily funny to them both, and they laughed.

"What else?" Hamil asked again.

"Isn't that enough? Why do you want to know, anyway?"

"Why shouldn't I want to know?" he countered unproductively. She looked exasperated.

"Oh, that's like you," she said.

"What's like me?"

"You won't commit yourself to anything. Oh, forget it." They walked on in silence. He knew what she meant – that he should have told her he was interested in her future for practical reasons; but he still felt the fear of chains, the worry of becoming like his father and mother. He wanted this summer at least, untrammelled, before he made up his mind about anything.

Later, however, when they were in bed and their good humour was restored, he brought up the subject again. It was warm, and they had only a single sheet over them. The windows were open and a cool, leaf-scented breeze blew on them. Olivia lay on her side with her lips against his shoulder, and with his free hand Hamil pulled her short, silky hair through his fingers in an absent gesture of love.

"Livia, what *do* you want to do?" he said.

"What does an English graduate with no particular training do? Teach? No thank you. I'd quite like to be a writer," she said, and it sounded so like a random decision that he snorted with laughter.

"What's so funny?" She sounded hurt. "People do write."

"Have you ever written anything before? What would you want to write, anyway? Novels, poems, plays, birthday cards?"

"Novels," she said, taking the question seriously. "All my poetry is juvenile and looks like staying that way – and you can't earn money at it anyway. I've written short stories before, but they don't satisfy. I want something bigger and longer—"

"That's my department," he said.

"Oh, you can mock," she said genially, "but I'm serious. I think I could be a good writer. I've made a start, and with practice I can only get better. One day I'll get it right – and then you'll see."

"You sound so confident," he said.

"So did you, about your music."

"Ah, but I didn't mean it."

"Didn't you? I believed you."

"Oh, I meant that it's what I *want* to do – but of course I can't be sure I'll be good enough."

"Oh, Hamil," she sighed, and pushed herself away from him to look up at him. "You can be as good as you want to be. You can do it, if only you don't let people stop you. That's what gets in the way. You meet someone—"

He pulled her to him and cuddled her roughly. "Who did you meet?" he asked.

He expected her to say, "You," from which point the rules of the game were simple and not at all obscure; but she didn't speak until he relaxed his hold on her, and then she said seriously, "You never commit yourself – and that's good, if you want to do all you say. But you mustn't ask others to commit themselves. That isn't fair. People need all the cover they can find, and if you insist on dragging them out on to the bare hillside, you'll have only yourself to blame if they snipe at you." There was no answer to that. "Sorry," she said. "Too serious. Forget it." Another pause. "Anyway – there's the answer to your question – part of it, at least."

"What question?"

"Where we'll be in ten years from now. You'll be playing with the Vienna Phil, and I'll be bumming round the world in a boat, writing a novel."

"When do you start?" he asked.

"As soon as I get Frances settled."

"Was she what you meant about meeting a person?" Hamil asked, a little shamefaced.

"Perhaps. In a way." She rolled over on to her back. "The change in her is remarkable. In a little while, she won't need me any more."

"Shall you be sad about that?" he asked curiously. She had sounded quite neutral, and he wondered if she could be so altruistic as to be glad when she was no longer necessary.

"Why should I be sad?"

"I suppose it's always tempting to attribute one's own mental processes to others. Other people's motives must be incomprehensible, simply by definition."

"True," she said abruptly. Then, as if she were changing the subject, "It's so hot! I don't envy you your trip to Mexico – it must be sweltering there. How long will you be away?"

"Six weeks."

"And when is it you leave?"

"You know that – next Tuesday. Why do you ask?"

"I just wondered," she said dismissively.

Afterwards he thought it over, and decided that perhaps other people's mental processes were not always obscure. She was right, he thought. He couldn't ask her for what he wanted without stepping out from behind his own screen. That would be hard to do, dangerous, and he needed time to pluck up his nerve, and the right occasion to do it; but between that conversation and the Tuesday of his departure he was working three sessions a day and didn't see her at all. He spoke to her most days, but he could hardly go into something so important and difficult on the phone. When he came back from Mexico he had a whole week in his diary without work: that would be the time to talk to her seriously and lay his cards on the table. He would ask her to marry him; and if he had his way, they would not get out of bed at all for the rest of the week.

Five

May 1966

"I'm not happy with this part," Ewan said, tapping his copy of the manuscript. His finger came straight from his mouth where he had been tearing at it greedily, and Hamil averted his eyes in distaste. Ewan had never bitten his fingernails as a child, as far as Hamil could remember. Now, when the nails were all gone, he bit his fingers, tearing skin from them until they bled. This, Ewan's own copy of the score, was pattered with little brown bloodstains amongst the crossings-out and alterations.

"Don't you think it's a little late in the day to be altering it again?" Hamil asked gently. His head was whirling. He had had a long day, rehearsing all morning, recording in the afternoon, and now working on the score with Ewan all evening. In addition, he had had to fit in his daily visit to Irene – though he had to admit Ewan was marvellous about going up to see her on all the occasions when Hamil couldn't make it. Irene didn't care too much for Ewan's company, but when you were flat on your back in hospital without being actually ill, any company was better than none.

Hamil's orchestra was to give the world première of Ewan's second symphony. His first symphony had been finished in record time under the supervision of Auerbach, and had received tremendous critical acclaim at its first performance in Edinburgh, with the great man himself taking the baton. It had since been played on the BBC and in capitals all over the world, including New York, and it was now being recorded, again by Hamil's orchestra, for release at the same time as the première of number two.

The second symphony, however, was proving more of a problem child, and there had been times over the last two years when Hamil had wondered if it would ever be finished.

"But darling, we have to have it absolutely right," Ewan said anxiously. Hamil grimaced. He had just got used to being called "darling" by his own brother, but he couldn't say he liked it. Besides, the room was heavy with smoke from Ewan's Turkish cigarettes and from those foul joss-sticks he insisted on burning when Hamil was away, and they had both been drinking more whisky lately than was good for them, all of which contributed to Hamil's feeling of ill temper.

"I don't think you'll ever have it exactly as you want it, for the simple reason that as long as you are alive, you keep changing and developing. If you change the work along with you, it'll never be finished. A piece of work surely has to be a—" He nearly said snapshot, but changed it at the last moment, having regard to Ewan's pride. "A portrait of where you are at one particular moment."

"How clever you are to think of that," Ewan said, delighted by this dynamic view of himself. "But look, just this little bit here . . . don't you think – now really – that it isn't quite right?"

Hamil wearily bent over the score and tried to sound it inside his head, while Ewan reached out for the bottle which was never far from his side during these sessions and gulped from it – they had long ago given up using glasses. In the kitchen, Hamil knew, was a pile of washing-up like something in a strip cartoon. From the point of view of peace and quiet, it was a good job that Irene happened to be in hospital while Ewan was staying in their flat, but it meant that the place disappeared daily under a fresh layer of silt.

"I can't think straight any more," Hamil said at last. "Give me that bottle and go and play it for me. I don't understand what you're getting at."

"OK," Ewan said, springing up. When it came to working on his music Ewan's energy was boundless. For the rest of the time, he was as limp and languid as a convalescent.

Hamil took a gulp of the whisky, feeling its burning passage blunted by repetition, and studied his brother as he settled himself at the piano and frowned over the music. Ewan had changed greatly in the last few years, and not for the better. He was thinner – so thin, in fact, that he appeared very tall. He had always had very white skin, and since he had the same dead-black, lamp-soot hair as Father and Fergus, the contrast had emphasised the pallor. Now, however, he definitely had a bad colour, and with the marks and shadows round his eyes he looked as though he had been very ill.

Hamil wondered how much of it was attributable to drink. Ewan drank enormously, but fitfully, not touching it for days, and then sinking a whole bottle of scotch in one session. When he did drink, it was in a greedy, snatching way, just as he smoked and savaged his shaking hands. He had bouts of frightful energy when he simply couldn't keep still but would walk up and down, talking and gesticulating. At other times he would lie around all day in an armchair with his eyes half shut, unable, it seemed, to speak or even eat.

It was, of course, proverbial that artists were moody, and Hamil naturally tended to attribute much of his brother's strangeness to the effort of composing, yet from time to time a cold finger of fear touched his thoughts and he wondered if his brother might be going mad. He had mentioned this to Irene, who had pooh-poohed it.

"He looks sick, I grant you, but that's only to be expected if he drinks as much as you say. You must have a word with him about that. It isn't right for a man of his age to look so old. But as for going mad – you mustn't dramatise so, Hamil. He puts on a show for you and you all encourage him."

Irene was of course naturally inclined to be irritable. She was pregnant, but was suffering from high blood-pressure, and since she had already lost one baby she had been ordered into hospital for bed rest. It was irksome to be in hospital anyway, but to be kept immobile – not even allowed up to the toilet – when she felt perfectly well was enough to try a saint.

Then, of course, she had not seen Ewan at home. When he visited Irene at the hospital he put on his best behaviour and was as charming as he knew how to be. To Ewan, Irene was a stranger, and he only relaxed in front of his family and close friends. Hamil tried to look at Ewan through Irene's eyes, but what he saw didn't change. He felt, uneasily, that there was something wrong with Ewan, but he had no idea how to come at it.

"This is the bit I mean," Ewan was saying, and played a passage rapidly on the piano. "The balance isn't right, is it? It's top-heavy."

Hamil made the effort and bent his mind to the task. It was immensely flattering that Ewan should come to him for advice, and immensely satisfying to be able, with his long experience of orchestras, to help with the technicalities of playing. But he couldn't say he fully understood what Ewan was trying to do, and he was always half in fear that he would say something that would make his brother turn on him with scorn for his ignorance.

"I think I have to change the scoring," Ewan said, rippling through sections of the passage over and over.

"I don't think you can do that now – not without restructuring the whole movement. Stop a minute; I can't think with you playing." Hamil stared at the lines, and the notes seemed to jump about like fleas. "Look, what about this? Here, in the six-eight, where you've got the first and second violins playing in thirds – how about if you brought the seconds in on the second beat of the bar? See what happens."

"What do you mean? Like this – syncopated?" Ewan tried it, playing one part and humming the other, and then looked up, excited. "That's absolutely it!" he cried. "All echoey, like water dripping – two taps, one here, one over there. Hollow and empty like an underground Gents'. But wait, even make it pizzicato! Yes! Plip plop. White tiles and urinals. This is how the world ends." He played it again, rocking with pleasure. "And then the bassoons and horns come in, heavy and mournful, with the plip-plopping over the top – and that links up with the mandolin entry. I'm a bloody genius!" He finished with a slamming chord and sat back. "But would they be able to do it? You can tell me, Hamil. We've one last rehearsal tomorrow – could they incorporate the change?"

"Of course," Hamil said. If it had to be done, they would do it. They were professionals, after all. "Now, if you'll take my advice, you'll leave it. The more you look over it, the more you're going to want to change. You'll lose the integrity if you mess about with it too much."

"Yes; you're right, of course. We'll leave it at that. Pass the bottle, will you, darling?"

Ewan left the piano and came across to sit on the floor, leaning against the armchair opposite Hamil, hugging the bottle to his chest and rocking backwards and forwards a little. His eyes were fixed on Hamil's face and if he were trying to divine his thoughts. At last he said, "Livy phoned today."

Hamil started, unable to prevent himself, thought it was not a form of the name he used even in his thoughts. He strove for a neutral tone.

"Did she?"

"Yes, with the arrangements for tomorrow. She's persuaded Mother not to come until tomorrow afternoon. You know Mother's first intention was to come down today, and spend this evening with us, *and* go to the rehearsal tomorrow?" He looked alarmed at the very thought, and took a gulp of whisky. It was so large as to burn even his throat, and he coughed.

"Go easy," Hamil said automatically. "Don't you ever get drunk? If I drank as much as you I'd be unconscious."

"What's this? What an admission from the great sinner of all time! Don't you know you're a legend back home?"

"Oh, shut up," Hamil said wearily.

"Well, it takes a lot more than one paltry bottle of scotch to get me drunk, I can tell you. Though there are things—" He looked absent for a moment, and Hamil stirred uneasily. He did not want to see into the dark places of Ewan's mind.

"But I was telling you about the arrangements," Ewan said suddenly, pulling himself back. "They're coming down tomorrow afternoon, and they've booked into a hotel in the Strand. They've even booked a room for me, she says, just in case – though she didn't say in case of what."

"So she won't be staying here?" Hamil asked, casually.

"No." Ewan narrowed his eyes. "So you'll be happy about that."

"Happy?"

"Not to have to clear up this pig-midden."

"Oh, yes, that – of course."

"And Mother's arranging a reception after the concert at the Waldorf." He pulled a face. "The only thing to be thankful for is that by the time everyone's got there, there won't be much time left. But – oh God—"

"It looks as though it's going to be a long day," Hamil said, not relishing the thought.

"Longer for me than for you," Ewan said bleakly. "Longer for me than for anyone. God help us, amen. Why on earth, tell me, did the Almighty see fit to create women?"

"I'm glad he did," Hamil protested mildly. "I know there's Mother, but on the other hand there's—"

"Olivia?" Ewan said. He was watching Hamil closely again.

"For one," he said. "Why – do you class Olivia with Mother?"

Ewan turned his head away fretfully.

"I don't know. Sometimes – it's all so hard. Are you happy, Hamil?"

"Happy?" Hamil was puzzled. "I don't know. I haven't thought about it. Happy in what way?"

"In your soul. Content. Do you know why you're here and where you're going? Are you happy with Irene, for instance? You didn't want this child, did you?"

"Who told you that?" Hamil said angrily. "I certainly never said anything of the sort."

"You're angry," Ewan observed. "Now that's interesting. You don't want the child, but you feel guilty about it – why is that?"

Hamil strove to be reasonable. "It isn't a matter of not wanting it. We just hadn't planned on having one just yet."

"Irene had."

"What are you talking about?"

"How do you think she got pregnant?"

"It was an accident."

"Balls," said Ewan, looking at him steadily.

Hamil stared. "Did she tell you that? That it wasn't an accident."

"Yes. In confidence, of course."

"Of course," Hamil said drily. "Well, thanks for telling me."

"You believe me?"

"Isn't it true?"

"In this case, yes, it does happen to be true," Ewan said, rising restlessly to his knees and then sitting down again. "I was just interested in your mental processes. I tell you something told to me in confidence, which proves I'm utterly untrustworthy, and yet you believe me rather than your wife. Shows a touching lack of faith in her, doesn't it?"

"Oh, for God's sake," Hamil exclaimed, standing up. "What am I supposed to say? What the hell has it to do with you anyway?"

He walked over to the window and stood there fuming, until, in the quietness, he began to wonder why he was angry. At last he said in a quiet voice, "Well, so I didn't want a child. What do you want to know now?"

"Why didn't you?"

"Want a child? Because – because I'm not ready. We haven't a house of our own, I haven't enough money, we couldn't give a child everything I'd want to give it." Ewan waited, and Hamil searched some more. "Because it would interfere with my career." None of this was the truth. The truth was that he didn't want Irene's child, but he couldn't say that to Ewan. It would be too disloyal. He didn't even want to admit it to himself. "Because it's a rotten world to be born into." This, a commonly spoken cant, would have to do.

"Do you really think that?" Ewan said. "Because it seems to me that the world is fantastic. It's people who are the problem. And in any case, however bad life is, it's better than the alternative."

"What alternative is there to life? Death? Well, at least that would be peaceful," Hamil said. His bad temper hadn't abated yet.

"Would it? Would it really? I wish I knew. Do you think there's anything after death, Hamil? Like we were taught as children – heaven and hell and all that?" Ewan's face turned up to him, white under the newly spiky haircut, the eyes bright and dull at the same time, like great energy at a great distance.

"I don't know about that," Hamil said. "Not literally, of course: They were tales for children. You have to work out something for yourself as you grow up."

"But if you work it out for yourself, it isn't true, is it?" Ewan folded his arms round his chest and rocked again. "You see, sometimes, when I'm writing, or listening to music, or maybe walking on the hills – something like that – I know there is a God, and that he made the world and me and the music I write. It all seems logical. It couldn't come from anywhere else. But when I think about it afterwards, in cold blood, I know that's all nonsense, and there's nothing but us. And, you see, I use the word 'know'. It is as certain as that. But how can I *know* two completely opposite things?"

"Maybe they are both true," Hamil said weakly. He didn't want to talk about this, now, with Ewan. It seemed too perilous.

"Do you believe in God?" Ewan insisted.

"I suppose so – or in some sort of superior being, anyway. Otherwise—"

"Yes, that's it – it's the 'otherwise' that's the trouble." He paused. "Livia doesn't, you know. She believes that there's just this life, and then you die, and that's it. So I asked her, if that's the case, what's the meaning of life, and she said—"

"What?"

"She said, 'Why should there be a meaning? I'm here because of a biological process. I shall one day stop, and be turned into putrefaction by another biological process. Where's the need for a meaning?' she said. And when she says it, it sounds so true. But, Hamil—"

Hamil waited in silence. Despite the peril he felt close to his brother, as if they were coming to a point where they might meet. If only Ewan could find the words. But Ewan was a musician, not a writer – words were not his strong point.

"It seems," he said at last, "all right to think that when you're young. But as you get older, and time runs out, what then? And when you come to die? I get this picture of her, dying, and struggling not to die, because this life was all she ever had. It seems so desolate to die like that."

He began to cry. Hamil went over to him, wondering how to comfort him, and Ewan grabbed him and pressed his face against Hamil's legs.

"I don't want to die like that," he sobbed. "Oh, I don't. That's why I keep on trying to prove it. Writing music. Because I'm afraid."

Holding Hamil, he rocked. When the sobs had died down, Hamil reached down and detached him, helped him up. "You're worn out," he said. "Go to bed."

"You help me," Ewan said in a muffled, childish voice. He draped himself over Hamil's shoulder, and Hamil led him away to the bedroom.

"You'll feel better after a sleep," he said. "Nothing ever seems so bad in the morning. It's a true thing I'm telling you, now. It'll be all right."

And Ewan seemed comforted, and lay down, and slept.

Hamil was sitting in the orchestra bar before the concert having a cup of coffee. He hadn't seen Ewan all day, not since the morning rehearsal had broken and Hamil had made his escape. He hadn't wanted to meet the family. He didn't know which of them he most dreaded having to face. In the back of his mind he felt guilty at deserting Ewan, but he reasoned that Ewan was going to have to meet them anyway, and there was no point in both of them suffering.

The final rehearsal had gone well. The late alteration had been incorporated without difficulty, and everyone seemed cheerfully optimistic, especially as one of the most important London critics had looked in for half an hour and had been seen to be nodding approvingly. Everything seemed set for a successful evening.

Now, in his white tie and tails, Hamil was waiting for the moment when his family would invade the bar with cries like birds of prey and he would be forced into the fringes of the limelight. He chatted lightly to a fellow musician with half his mind elsewhere and his cup in his hand, until he was arrested in mid-flow by Olivia, alone, standing by his chair.

He stared up at her, and felt his heart sink at her expression. He knew what it was without being told.

"Hamil, will you come outside a moment? I have to speak with you."

She was beautiful, and not his wife, and there were some broad grins on faces as he followed her outside. In the comparative privacy of the corridor she turned to him.

"It's Ewan."

"I guessed it. What is he – drunk?"

"He's disappeared. Oh, I knew there was something brewing. I pretty well suspected he'd work a flanker of some sort. Fergus was supposed to keep tabs on him – there are some places I can't follow him, obviously. Well, Fergus muffed it. Ewan gave him the slip, and now, God knows where he is."

"Does Mother know?" Hamil asked.

"Not yet, but she soon will. I shan't be here to see her reaction, thank God. I'm going out now to find him."

"In the whole of London? Don't be ridiculous!" Hamil exclaimed. "You'd never find him. You wouldn't know where to start looking."

"I'll find him," she said grimly. "I know where to look. The point is, by the time I find him he may not be fit to go back to the hotel. Can I take him to your place?"

"I suppose so," he said, taken aback.

"Don't be thick, Hamil," she said impatiently. "I mean, are you alone there?"

"Irene's still in hospital. Yes – yes, I am alone." He caught the tail of her question at last, and realised she had wondered if he already had another woman keeping Irene's seat warm for her. He had hardly time to resent it.

Olivia said quickly, "One more thing – does he have his own key?"

"Yes – I gave him a spare, so he should have it with him. But I'll wait up anyway. I won't go to the party – I'll go straight home."

Some of the strain slid momentarily out of her face.

"Bless you for that," she said, and then she was gone, before he could ask her where she was going to start looking, or whether she was going to change out of her evening dress first.

It was nearly midnight when scuffling and banging outside the door woke him from a fitful doze, and he hurried to open it. Livia stood there, supporting Ewan with her arm round his waist and his arm over her shoulder. Ewan's eyes were closed but for a slit. His face was dead white, his clothes rumpled. Livia was wearing a skirt and jumper – she had obviously changed before initiating her search.

"Thank heaven you're back," Hamil said. "I was getting worried."

He tried to help her, but she grunted and said, "Just move aside, I can manage." She inched forward, half carrying, half dragging Ewan. She had evidently done this before, for she was taking most of his weight by pulling down on the arm that hung over her shoulder, so that Ewan's feet were hardly touching the ground. When he was finally in a position to help her, Hamil was astonished by how much of Ewan's weight she was taking.

"Let's get him to bed," she said through her teeth.

"Oh yes, of course – this way. Can I help you now?"

"Yes; take the other side. Get his arm over you like this. Lucky he's so skinny."

Together they shuffled down the hall with their animated burden, and worked their way into the room that Ewan had been using.

"Sit him on the bed – right – easy."

"What's wrong with him?" Hamil found time to ask. He had never seen anyone look quite so ill.

"Only drink, thank God. Here, hold him up a minute – don't let him lie down." She left Hamil propping his comatose brother in a sitting position and returned moments later with a milk bottle full of water.

"One pint of water," she said. "Keep holding him up. Right – down she goes." She propped his head up with one hand while with the other she guided the bottle to Ewan's lips. Ewan's eyes parted a fraction and he murmured fretfully, but he began to swallow, and once having started he continued obediently until the bottle was empty. The mere sight made Hamil feel bloated.

"What—?" he began.

"Aid against dehydration. Alcohol is hygroscopic, draws all the water out of your tissues. Hence the hangover. All right, lay him down now."

With Hamil's help she took off his socks, loosened his trousers, undid the buttons at the neck of his shirt. "Helps circulation," she explained. "Cover him up well, and we'll open the windows. A hangover is ninety per cent dehydration and ten per cent lack of oxygen. All right," at length. "He'll do now. Let's leave him. Oh – have you got a washing-up bowl, or something like that?"

"In the kitchen," Hamil said, with a questioning look.

"Better leave it beside the bed just in case. If he wakes, he'll probably vomit."

Ewan was already unconscious – it hardly seemed like sleep – and made no sound or movement as they went out, leaving the door slightly ajar.

In the lighted sitting room she flopped into an armchair and passed a hand across her eyes.

"Can I get you anything?" Hamil asked her, rather awkwardly. After what he had just witnessed he hardly liked to offer her a drink.

"Oh, dear Hamil, how kind you are. I'd love some coffee, if you could manage it."

"Something to eat?"

"Not now – I couldn't. Perhaps later."

He put the kettle on, and hurried back to her. She was straightening her clothes and setting her hair to rights.

"You seem," he said a little wryly, "almost professional. Do you have to do that sort of thing often?"

"Often enough," she said. "It's your mother – she won't leave him alone. She gets him worked up and – oh, what's the use? I've said it all so often I'm sick of hearing myself talk. And I shouldn't talk about her in front of you. Sorry." She made a vague gesture of wiping out what she had said.

"What did you mean, it's only drink?" he asked. "Isn't it usually drink?"

"Sometimes. Sometimes it's other things. On the whole, I prefer the drink. Drunks I know how to handle. Hallucinations I can't cope with."

"Drugs?"

"Hm," she grunted, leaning her head back in the chair and closing her eyes. "I had a job getting him back. Two taxis wouldn't take us, so we walked a good part of the way. Otherwise I'd have been back sooner."

"How did you know where to look?" Hamil was still curious about this point.

"There are only a certain number of places he would go. Bars where his sort collect."

She didn't want to elaborate on that point, and for a while there was silence. Her eyes were still closed, and he was able to indulge himself with studying her for a while. She seemed unchanged, except that she looked tired, and having her here, being alone with her in his own flat again, made him feel that time had not passed and that they were still what they had been to each other during that happy summer.

He didn't want to think about the difference, because it had been so largely of his own making. If he had not delayed, if he had taken the bold path, made the decision – but he had not. Wretched procrastinator that he was – coward, trimmer, call it what you will – he had waited until he got back from Mexico. It was his old, bad habit of waiting for Fate to decide things for him. And instead, Fate had decided against him. When he came back from Mexico, it was already too late. Without any assurance from him, left alone and thrown on her own resources, she had been cornered, trapped, committed. He had lost his chance.

But for the moment it was possible to forget that she was married to Ewan and he was married to Irene. Those facts could be obliterated by the sheer familiarity of the situation, and by the impossibility of ever imagining her in bed with anyone else.

Perhaps she felt something of the same, for she opened her eyes and said, "We meet again – in the aspect, at least, of strangers. How did the concert go? One ought to ask these questions."

"It went well, I thought. The audience seemed enthusiastic, if that means anything. And the conductor seemed pleased."

"I was sorry to miss it. He's a good composer, isn't he? I

wanted to hear you play, too: he wrote you in ten bars, I understand. I'd have liked to hear that, to see if you're as brilliant as you were – but of course you are. So it went well – that's good."

"But why does he have to go and get drunk?" Hamil protested. "I don't understand it. He's been drinking all week, but though what he takes in would put the average man under the table, he's never been drunk."

"I think it's just that he can't stand the strain of being a celebrity," she said with a wry face. "At normal times he can live with himself because he just isn't introspective enough to upset himself. But when something like this happens his mother starts on at him about how famous and important he is and how the world will rock when he so much as sneezes, and he just can't take it. She's been working him up all afternoon. I told her to leave him alone, but she just smiles at me and says she is his mother after all, and she ought to understand him better than me, considering how long she's known him. And then she laughs – you know the way she does." She imitated his mother to perfection, and Hamil himself almost laughed, though it was sad rather than funny. "The trouble is she sees herself as the great patron of the arts – the great lady inspiring the artist. Ideally she'd have liked to be the nude model-mistress of a celebrated painter. As it is, she isn't averse to being the power behind a musician or two."

Hamil, remembering her affairs with members of his own orchestra, nodded painfully.

"Of course," Olivia went on, "she doesn't know about the horrible group he goes around with in Edinburgh. I was invited once, but never again. I showed them too clearly what I thought of them. Ewan says he likes them because they're the only ones who understand him properly. They don't, of course – they just like his money. He has plenty of *that*, at least; enough to keep them all in drink. Or worse."

She rubbed her eyes wearily.

"Do you want to go to bed?" he asked her.

"No, I don't think I could bear it," she said. "Talk to me, Hamil; tell me about your life, keep me amused. I don't want to think any more. Talk to me about anything except your family – I suppose I ought to say *my* family, now. All the family I have, at any rate."

"I never did know anything about your family," Hamil said, at a loss for a subject. The only thing he wanted to do was to take her to his bed and hold her, but that was out of the question now. "I seem to remember someone once telling me you had a brother, but that's all I can remember."

"I wonder who could have told you that," she said, seeming wryly amused. Hamil racked his brains.

"It seems strange, but I have a kind of idea it was my father," he said, puzzled at the idea himself.

"Well, I did have a brother, but he was killed years back."

"Oh, I'm sorry. Not a happy choice of subject."

"It's all right, it doesn't hurt now. He was much older than me, and it was a long time ago."

"How did it happen?"

"He was a test pilot for a firm of aircraft manufacturers. He flew his plane into the side of Biggin Hill."

"An accident?"

"Apparently not. There was nothing wrong with the aircraft. I think he'd just had enough – done everything he'd ever wanted to do, and didn't want to do anything again. So that was the only thing left to try." A brief silence. "I expect he was nuts," she said casually. "So you see I'm well qualified to deal with – damn and blast, I've brought the subject round to your brother again."

"It's strange the way you refer to him as my brother and not as your husband," Hamil said.

"That's a dangerous subject to get on to," she warned.

"It's a hard one to keep off," Hamil admitted.

"Oh, to hell with the Strathearn family," she said with an

attempt at lightness. "One day, one day, I shall buy a boat and sail round the world, and write a book about it."

"It's been done," Hamil cautioned her.

"So what? Chippendale didn't stop because the world was full of chairs."

Hamil laughed. "That's different."

"Not different at all," she said stoutly. "Anyway, I shall write it, even if no one wants to read it. That's the least of my problems, as Oscar Wilde said when he was soaping himself in the shower."

"Livia, when you buy your boat and go round the world, can I come with you?"

"I'll tell you something, Hamil," she said seriously. "When that day comes, I shall come and ask you. I shall say, 'The boat's anchored just over there, and I'm all ready to go. How about it, buddy?' And do you know what you'll say?"

"What?" he asked, amused.

"You'll say, 'I'm frightfully sorry, but I've got something rather important on tomorrow – could we make it the day after? Or next week?' And you won't come with me." She shook her head sadly. "It gets you in the end, you know."

"What does?"

"Middle age."

Over coffee and more coffee they talked through the night until dawn broke over the grimy roofs of Notting Hill and Ewan woke heavily in the next room and called for Livia. It was a strange night, fantastic in recollection, a sort of nowhere night like the middle step of a flight, exactly half-way between one state of existence and another. Hamil thought of it afterwards as the night when he finally understood how he felt about Olivia, but it was, after all, the kind of night that has that sort of thing said about it afterwards. Still, it might have been true.

Six

December 1968

Through the fragile daylight of another Christmas Eve Hamil drove northwards, up the A1. So little daylight – almost the shortest day – and what remained was fitful, inadequate for the purpose. Irene, beside him, had talked at first, but as his driving grew more frantic and she grew more tired and afraid, she relapsed into a tense, exhausted silence, unable to sleep, nor to take her eyes off the grey road and grey sky ahead of her. She had not been well since the birth of their second baby, and she clung to her infirmity as a means to secure at least some of the attention she needed.

On the back seat the two babies slept, and sometimes cried. Their crying exhausted both Irene and Hamil, so that they would exchange brief, desperate glances as they keyed themselves up for the distance to the next lay-by. The children held them together and kept them apart like the pull of equal and opposite forces. They were heavy between their parents like a tacit admission. Irene had wanted them to fill the gap Hamil's absence left, to give her companionship and a sense of purpose. Hamil had fathered the first in a fit of jealous misery over Olivia, and the second – born only a year after the first – to justify that first criminal error. They might have been delightful children, but their intolerable significance blinded him to any other aspect of their existence.

He drove faster the further north he went. He was conscious of a growing, unloosening joy at the achievement of every mile nearer to Olivia. He longed only to see her again, was filled with a wild terror at the thought of wasting any possible minute of her company. Of course, they would not be alone together – all the family was gathering for one of those deadly family Christmases that Mother loved to organise – but he was so starved of her presence, of the attainment of any level of love, that to be with her was, for the moment, all he desired.

That he had no guilt, even with Irene beside him, was a monument to his upbringing: the selfishness of a member of a large family – necessary to the middle one of five – combined with the irresponsibility engendered by his mother's interference and his father's indifference.

That he was aware of feeling no guilt was the achievement of his freedom. He left so much of himself behind with his family that what he brought with him was a source of wonder to him. Each trick of individuality won from the covering blandness of the shared name he regarded with an involuted pride. He was to himself of absorbing interest, but it was not the sort of self-regard that sustained. His perpetual analysis only left him more desperately lonely. He wanted someone with whom to share his watch over his own development.

He had, of course, a great many men friends. He was the sort of man who would always have male intimates – the sort of friends who, in battle, would give their lives for each other. Working as he did, as one of a closely knit group of men, slightly cut off from the outside world, he found a measure of happiness, but the friendship of men left him always aware of a shortfall. There was a level of communion that he missed.

He did not consciously connect his feeling of hunger with sex. He had sex with Irene, of course, and with one or two other women when the opportunity presented itself – orchestras always attracted their share of, mostly female, fans. There were occasions when he was aware that the satisfaction of the act was imperfect and temporary, but at those times he mentally attributed the blame to some physical shortcoming in himself or his partners. Still, he wanted, though he appreciated it only vaguely with the back of his mind, a companion. It did not occur to him to make a companion of his wife or his mistresses. He saw them as women, not as people.

But Olivia burned clear and steady in one corner of his mind, the woman for whom he had made an exception. His desire for her over the years had grown and developed, flourishing in his loneliness and sending out shoots and suckers into every corner of his consciousness. Unattainable, she represented to him the fulfilment of his loneliness. Since there was obviously no chance of putting his love to the test and disappointing it, he liked to think that, had they married, everything would have been all right.

Everything had not been all right in the past eighteen months, and seemed to be getting worse. He was tired, so tired that only the longing to see Livia had tempted him to drive so far to spend his paltry time off. Working with the orchestra was exhausting when you worked every session, as Hamil did – working often fourteen hours a day and seven days a week. He admitted privately the justice of Irene's complaints that he smoked and drank too much, but he knew nevertheless that it was the only way he could cope with the strain of the work.

And it was not possible to slacken off. Thought he made what he might have called a "decent screw", it was not a guaranteed salary but depended entirely on how much work he did; and his living expenses grew heavier all the time. There was the mortgage of the flat, insurance, the car, the children – who seemed to have arrived trailing not so much clouds of glory but strings of bills; and Irene was not a good manager. He did not want her to be – his inherited pride told him that his wife should not need to be a good manager – but to keep one step ahead of the financial demands he had to work all the sessions he was offered.

And he had suffered a disappointment, for the chance had come and gone of joining the German ensemble, which had been his ambition. Sheer tiredness and pressure of work was his excuse – he had so little time to practise his audition pieces, so little time to brush up his technique – but an inner voice hinted to him that he had not applied for the position because he was afraid of not getting it. He did not want to know that he was not good enough to pass the audition. Yet even having not tried for it, the sense of failure sat heavy on him.

But if he was not good enough, he could *be* good enough, if he put his mind to it. He knew that was true – about his work he was incurably honest, even if only to himself. It was putting his mind to it that was the problem. What was it Livia had said? "I can do what I want, but I can't want what I want." To what extent, he wondered, did he encumber himself with the mundane burdens of family and material security to avoid having to make the effort to be an artist? He had an idea that it would be both more and less lonely in those rarefied heights, and he was not sure he could sustain the extraordinary rapture he imagined would take the place of his familiar thoughts.

After all, look at Ewan. That was the point, wasn't it? He had Ewan before him as an example, and to the extent that he understood Ewan's terror of himself, he understood Livia for marrying him. His foot inched down again on the accelerator at the thought of her, and Irene stirred stiffly and unhappily on the seat beside him. He felt her movement and the exact degree of discomfort she sustained, but outwardly he ignored her. He drove on, his mind richly peopled with his family and himself, to the mounting anticipation and the darkening horizon.

Christmas Eve: dark so early in Edinburgh that the evening and night were timeless. The family grouped and regrouped in drawing room and kitchen and morning room and in the spaces in between, each group a new permutation and each conversation a slightly variant blend of all the things to be said. It was good that there were so many of them, and so much to do – Mother was obsessively hospitable, seeing herself in the role of great society hostess; enjoying only the power of providing and assembling, enjoying nothing of the result herself. But the sheer plurality ensured that no one would be too greatly displeased nor too rawly exposed.

Douglass was there, with Morton and her two children – a Douglass grown, despite her worldly success, into a typical Edinburgh matron, with a rigid propriety and a steely beauty that would keep her looking much the same – never older, certainly never younger – until widowhood. She treated her husband with the same frigid concern that she showed to her children, and Hamil remembered with regret that fierce tenderness she had shown the first time she brought him home. Yet, she had said, she had never loved him, so perhaps it was not impossible that a marriage could end well.

Douglass took over responsibility for Irene and for Hamil's children with a prompt efficiency, and Irene visibly relaxed. Theirs was to be a domestic and medical Christmas. When they were not preparing food or clearing away meals they discussed their respective confinements and the health of Mr Strathearn, who had been suffering from an unspecified ailment. Hamil had an idea that they discussed him, too, for he caught the occasional glance in his direction. His excessive drinking, probably, and his chances of a breakdown.

Frances and Ewan raced about the house like children, noisy and excited, so that Hamil was reminded of Christmas Eves in the past when they were children in actual fact. Ewan's high spirits seemed to Hamil almost hysterical. He had been working, his father said, very hard all week and the noise was probably only letting off steam, but to Hamil it seemed more ominous than that. There was, too, something slightly ominous to him in the kindly interest Mr Strathearn was showing in everyone's concerns. It was not like him, and anything out of the ordinary was bound to provoke anxiety in the state Hamil was in.

His father made little of his illness. It was nothing but advancing age, he said. "A few aches and pains, a little stiffness, a little failure of the digestive system – all to be expected." This in itself was out of character, for Hamil could not remember a time when his father had discussed with him any personal subject. He made no allowance for the fact that he himself was growing up, and could perhaps with justice be confided in. To Hamil his parents were always his parents, just as women were women – they were more functional than real, and recognised by certain large, well-printed labels.

"Have you seen a doctor?" he asked automatically, and his father looked at him quizzically.

"No," he said, and his expression seemed to imply, "Now what on earth are you going to say next?"

Hamil strove for neutral ground, and failed. "Where are the others? Fergus, I mean, and—" He was afraid to say her name, afraid he could not pronounce it without giving himself away.

"Olivia? They've gone on some necessary social visits – duty calls, you might say. I expect they will be back rather late."

Hamil considered the implications of duty calls that could be fulfilled by the unexpected combination of Olivia and Fergus. "Relatives?" he hazarded.

"Clients," his father told him with satisfaction at having held him off. "Once, of course, we would have invited them all here for sherry, but that was when you were all young enough to be sent to bed at seven. And when you'd be likely to stay there."

"But why Olivia?" Hamil persisted, dangerously.

His father's attention was flagging, and he lifted the book he was holding on his knee in a suggestive way. "Like all of us," he said, "she needs a break from time to time."

He let his gaze drop to the page as if by accident. Break from what? Hamil wondered; but he understood that the audience was at an end, and in any case he could supply the answer for himself. What surprised him was not that his father could be so perceptive, for he had always thought of him as being the silent observer on the outskirts of the family, but that he should express it. *But then,* Hamil thought, *I have no experience at all of Livia's relationship with my father – none at all.*

It was late when they came in, so late that those who were going to Midnight Mass had already left. Irene had gone to bed. The lack of sufficient space meant that she and Hamil were sleeping apart – Douglass and Morton were having the only available double bed – and Irene's relief was great enough to be apparent. Hamil was amused and a little touched that she should be taking a holiday from him as well as from the babies. It seemed in this house she could yield up all responsibility and be again as she had been during their engagement, but with one difference: now she did not come to say goodnight to him.

Hamil wandered restlessly around the house, unable to settle in any room. The house seemed small to him, smaller than in his memories, and shabbier, without the theatrical glamour he remembered with such delight. He wondered if it were so in fact, or if his feelings were affecting him, but in any case, there seemed no comfort here for him. Where once he could have settled in a familiar corner with a book, or simply with a drink and his thoughts, now he paced and prowled, turning every now and then to the window that looked out on the street. He would twitch the curtain aside and stare at the oblique slice of the road outside that was more familiar to him than his own face, so familiar that he barely saw it. He seemed in retrospect to have spent half a lifetime staring at that section of road, the boundary of his prison. Though he had left it years since, the boundary remained in his mind and held him still.

Would she be changed, as the others were? Older, less extraordinary? Would she have changed towards him, either for better or worse? What horrible shocks would his observation store up for him? And when he heard, in the stillness of the night, the footsteps coming up the stairs, two sets only, he did not go forward to open the door and greet them, but stood by the window, holding the curtain as if he might want to hide behind it.

There were voices, footsteps, a laugh, indeterminate noises, and then the door opened and they came in, Fergus and Olivia. He stayed quite still where he was, as if any movement might shatter him. He could hardly bear to find out she was unchanged; even that much knowledge was past endurance.

They both called out greetings to him, and Olivia went straight over to his father, who was reading in the wing-backed chair by the fire, and kissed his cheek and asked him how he did. Then she took a step towards Hamil and stopped.

"Well?" she said.

He met her eyes reluctantly.

"Well what?"

What significances might have passed between them he never knew. She paused to make sure of her reply, but Fergus took advantage of the pause and came over to shake Hamil's hand – an odd, alien gesture for Fergus – and ask him enthusiastically how he was.

"Did you have a good journey?"

"Tiring," he found himself answering. "Irene's gone to bed, she was so exhausted."

"We were sorry not to have been here to meet you, but there were various people we had to visit: important clients and assorted bigwigs. You know the sort of thing." The "we" was proprietary, the verbal equivalent of an arm around the shoulders.

Livia's eyes never left Hamil's face, but he addressed himself to Fergus.

"You and Olivia?"

"Who else?" he said reasonably. "Mother never would, and Frances hasn't two words to rub together in company. Have you had a drink?"

"I'll go to bed now that you're back," Mr Strathearn interrupted. He stood up carefully and looked from Hamil to Fergus with an expression of satisfaction. "At least the two of you—" he began, and stopped abruptly. "Well, goodnight. Olivia, my dear—"

She stepped forward to be kissed, and the three of them watched him go through the door, closing it behind him.

"How bad is he?" Hamil asked abruptly.

Fergus looked at Olivia, as if medical analysis was a woman's business.

"Who knows?" she said lightly. "He won't tell anyone. It's his business, anyway."

"Have you had a drink?" Fergus asked again, quickly, as if he were covering up for her. Hamil had the impression that they had quarrelled on that point before, and the degree of intimacy thus implied distanced him again. But after all, she and Ewan had been living here. He was very much the visitor.

"Several," he answered. "But I'll have another."

"Whisky? And you, Olivia?"

At least he didn't use any of the pet names. Like conspirators they stood in silence until Fergus, too, had left the room, and then Livia turned to him with a sigh.

"I'm glad to see you again," she said.

He swallowed. "How are you?"

"Bearing up, but badly," she said, taking a leap into intimacy. Like him, she walked to the window and looked out, the motion of a thing caged, a purely involuntary gesture. "There's going to be trouble soon. Oh Hamil" – she turned to him quickly – "why can't people just leave each other alone?"

"It wouldn't do," he said. "There'd be no point in anything. Do you leave people alone?"

"No, of course not. You're quite right. But we need to get away. I wish we all lived in London."

"London isn't such a bed of roses," he said quickly.

She considered him. "You've had bad news?"

"I didn't get that place I was after."

"Oh, Hamil! What happened?"

Now was the time to be honest. Since he had to tell her the truth, he might find out what the truth was. He met her eyes.

"Nothing at all happened. I didn't go for the audition. I was afraid of making a mess of it. But I think at heart I didn't really want to get the place. Too much of a risk, I suppose."

"Your present position is not without risk," she pointed out. "A trumpet player lives on the line, always. If you make a mess of things, you can't hide in the section."

"True. But it's a risk I'm used to. The ensemble was an unknown factor. And then there's Irene and the children."

"Yes, there is, isn't there," she said thoughtfully. "Did you know your father has a villa in Spain?"

"No," he said, astonished.

"He owns quite a lot of property, in Edinburgh mostly, but also this villa . . . I want to take Ewan there."

Her remark had not been a non-sequitur. That was the other part of the equation. As there was Irene, so there was Ewan – only more so, for Ewan was his as well as hers, doubly impossible ever to remove from the picture.

"Why?"

"I have to get him away from Edinburgh, before he breaks up completely. The way things are here it's impossible for him to work. He'll be able to work there, without distractions."

"What will Mother say?"

"I think after Christmas she will let him go," she said grimly. "There's going to be trouble, and she'll be glad to get rid of him for a while."

"What sort of trouble?" he asked, but at that moment Fergus came back in with the drinks.

"Not talking about me, I hope?" he said cheerily as they fell silent.

"Did you want us to?" Hamil countered. He regarded his brother with faint surprise. There seemed something very different about him, a sort of ponderous gaiety, as if he were a man twice his age putting on the motley for the first time. Fergus had always been grave and quiet, in his father's shadow; weighted with the vast complexity of the Law, with paternal expectations, with the responsibility of the family business that supplied all their various necessities. Too much had always been expected of him for him to be light; and, like their father, he had stood outside the brightly coloured artistic circus in which the rest of them lived and moved. Hamil had sometimes – he admitted it to himself guiltily – confounded Fergus and Father in his mind and made them one. But as the granite monolith of his father seemed to be softening and blurring, Fergus seemed to be moving more into the foreground, becoming better delineated. Was that him, Hamil, or was that Fergus?

"Well, here's to us," Fergus said, passing the tumblers out.

"Wha's like us?" Hamil replied obediently, though with an effort.

"Gae few—"

"An' they're a' deid," Livia finished. They drank.

"That's good," Fergus commented. "We've drunk nothing but sherry all night."

"Sassenachs!" Olivia laughed. "Did you bring in the bottle?"

"Of course I did – what do you take me for?" Fergus retorted. They refilled their glasses, and something like festivity crept into their company – crept cautiously, like a cursed dog. "Did you know we've been teaching Olivia to play the piano?"

"No. There seems to be a lot I don't know. The news doesn't reach me in my outpost of the empire. What can she play?"

"I'll show you," she said. Her face alight with fun, she sat down at the great old piano and burst into "Chopsticks".

Fergus made a gesture of shutting the lid on her fingers and said, "Stop it! Play properly; don't shame us."

"All right," she said, and after a pause began to play the lullaby from Fauré's *Dolly Suite*. "I asked to learn it," she said when she had finished the opening phrases. "It takes me back to my childhood. Oh yes, Hamil, even I had a childhood."

"You told me once that nothing had happened to you before you came here," he replied.

The focus of the room contracted sharply so that there was

only himself and Livia, a few feet apart: he standing, she sitting at the piano. The fire cracked and spat in the sudden silence. Livia picked up her glass and raised it to him, and he repeated her gesture and drank the living taste of memory. *Whatever happens, remember this.*

"I wanted to think that," she said. "But of course, you never outlive your past, though you may forget it. But everything good that's ever happened to me has happened since then, that's true. And the best is yet to come."

"Let's have one more drink before Mother gets back," Fergus said, and the room receded into normality again.

"She won't like us being festive without her," Olivia said. "That was partly why we stayed out so long, so that we wouldn't have to go to Midnight Mass. How did you get out of it?"

"She didn't ask me," Hamil said cheerfully.

"Mother wouldn't ask Hamil," Fergus told her as if amazed by her stupidity. "Everyone knows Hamil does what he wants and when he wants. He's the playboy of the western world, as free as air; nobody ties him down."

Which goes to show, Hamil thought, *by how much a reputation can outlive the truth.*

They talked happily until the return of the church party broke them up. Hamil found himself enjoying his brother's company, and, perhaps with justice, attributed the humanising process to Olivia. The pleasant talk, the firelight, the whisky and being with Livia again made a bright, soft place in his memory, and it was that part of the Christmas he remembered best in retrospect, though it lasted such a short while.

The church party arrived, minus Ewan. He had run on ahead, apparently, saying he felt the cold, and should have been home long ago, but somewhere between the church and the house he had gone astray. Hamil, glancing at Livia, saw she had expected this. He remembered her words – that there was going to be trouble – and he thought that perhaps to some extent she had allowed it, that she could have prevented it.

Whether she could have or not, it became obvious to Hamil that his mother believed Olivia had engineered the escape. Much became clear to Hamil during the course of that unhappy Christmas when the intricacy of his family's relationships with Olivia were revealed to him. His mother believed Olivia to be plotting and conniving with Ewan against her, but the thing that astonished Hamil was that she appeared to be afraid of Olivia. That accounted for some of his father's expansion, then, and for the intimacy between Fergus and Olivia. The strands were so deeply entangled in the person who had started merely as "Frances's friend" that there was no need to wonder why she had made that pathetic gesture of going to the window. They all depended on her in some way – Hamil was not alone in that.

The only person whose relationship with her he had no chance to study was Ewan, and for that he was glad. Whether Ewan turned out to love her a great deal or very little or not at all, it was bound to be painful to Hamil. He would rather not know anything about Ewan's feelings for his wife, for whatever the answer was, its very certainty would make it the worst possible answer to bear.

Seven

September 1970

The villa was built on a promontory at the end of a road that led nowhere else. To the road it presented its blank, pink-washed face across a concrete apron marked with car tyres. Its grounds were on the other side, terraced and stepped down to the sea which crawled, blue and impersonal, fifty feet below.

As he got out of the taxi, the sun struck the top of his head like a brass cymbal. The air was full of the hot rich odour of dust, and alien plant-smells: resin and flowers and the spiky tang of sea vegetation. The quality of the light was strange too, oddly opaque after the quartz clarity of the northern light he had been born into, and he found it increasingly difficult to believe that he was here – that *here* was here, that he was not dreaming.

Hamil would not allow himself to regret the impulse which brought him here, though he had already in his mind played out the scene of retribution which would face him when he returned to reality. The summer tour had exhausted him; the pressure of work, the climate, the endless travelling, the strange food and the inevitable excess of drink had brought him to the stage when he was in measurably worse condition than any of his colleagues. An attack of Montezuma's revenge had been the last straw, precipitating a crisis. There were only two concerts left, and a hastily convened meeting of the board and the conductor had decided that with a very small alteration to the programme they could manage with only two trumpets for those, so that Hamil could be sent home early, to rest.

To rest. Wearily his mind considered the possibility. Irene and the children. Irene after three weeks alone with the children. The children after three weeks in the flat, in summer, with Irene, without him. He knew that he ought not to consider the prospect from his own viewpoint alone, but he had never succeeded in committing himself wholeheartedly to Irene, and his sense of responsibility towards what he must now, he supposed, consider as his family was at best patchy. He did not want to spend time with her, with them. His work was his passion, and his chosen profession had made them more of a financial burden than an emotional one, had enabled him so far to avoid any confrontation of the particular problem they should have been to him.

And now, at the last moment, he had chickened out. He had skipped plane and had run for it, and after a long journey that already seemed to him a heat-hallucination, he had arrived at the only place he could think of, the only door in the world that would admit him with welcome. How much of a welcome he could not be sure, but he would be able to rest here.

He crossed the anvil of the concrete apron and passed through the wicket into the shade that lay like well-water along the side of the house. It was the time of day when everyone ought to be sleeping under nets indoors, but as he reached the front of the house he heard the sound of a piano being played.

No, not being played – that was too definite a word for the hesitant non-sequence of notes he could hear. It was almost like someone tuning. One note was played, then another, some right hand and some left, and then several together. He stood, still in the shade of the house, listening as, very slowly, the first phrases of *Für Elise* were assembled.

He knew then who it must be. In the same way, phrase by phrase, she had been taught the Fauré lullaby, as a parrot is taught to recite poetry.

The terrace, weighted with bougainvillaea, had in its darkness windows open, and a louvred double door in place of a French window leading into the dim room beyond. The piano was at the far side, away from any ray of the destructive sun, and Olivia was there alone – teaching herself from the music, note by painful note. She looked up, startled at his appearance. She was crying. The breath of surprise she drew vibrated as it coincided with a sob.

Her crying distressed Hamil, and embarrassed him. He did not know whether to refer to it or not, whether to ask questions or to ignore the tears with a cheerful greeting. She looked at him as he crossed the room, and obviously wanted to speak but could not. He reached the piano where she sat, and, unable to touch her, rested his hands helplessly on the piano top. Her face was ugly with the effort to restrain her tears. He looked round him uneasily.

"Are you alone?"

She nodded, unable to speak. After a moment she put her hands up to her face, wiping at the tears with a futile gesture, and then stared at her wet hands, not knowing what to do with them. He found her his handkerchief, ashamed that it was so dirty and crumpled, and she folded it carefully to the cleanest place before wiping her face on it. He had never seen anyone cry so freely and copiously. The tears flowed from her eyes like blood from a face wound, and as fast as she wiped the tears away, they were replaced.

At last she abandoned the effort and put her head down in her arms. Released from the sight of her, he moved round the piano, edged her off the stool and sat down himself, taking her on to his lap. She moved heavily, like a drunken thing, putting her arms round his neck and her face on his shoulder. He felt the tears soaking hot through his shirt, but his arms round her body felt good to him. There was an enormous physical relief in touching her.

At last she stopped crying and grew still, and he became aware of his own physical arousal, and wondered what to do about it.

Would she notice? If he kept very still, perhaps she would not. What would she think of him, aroused in the midst of her grief?

He tried not to shift uncomfortably and at last said, to distract her, "Poor Livia. What was all that for?"

"It was the music that started it," she said unevenly, still hitching. "I can't play the piano, and the frustration made me cry."

"But it wasn't for that you were crying. What is it, darling? Tell me."

She wiped the tears from her face with the back of her hand, a touchingly childish gesture. Tenderness reinforced his lust for her, and as she looked at last into his face at such close quarters, he felt she must read it in his expression as well as feel it through his clothes.

"Oh Hamil, you must have known. I've been here all alone since last night, and even though yesterday I would have killed him rather than have to spend another day in his company, by this morning I was so lonely I wanted to die. And just when I need you most, you turn up on the doorstep like a ghost." She put her wet hand against his cheek. "I hope to God I'm not dreaming this. I'm not dreaming, am I? You are really here?"

"Very much here," he said. "But where are the others?"

"Switzerland," she said abruptly. She took a shuddering breath and pulled herself close to him, and he folded his arms round her again, tightly, for comfort. "Ewan's been very bad recently," she went on, her voice muffled. "He's been working very hard, and when he stops working, he goes on a bender. Usually it only lasts a day or two, and then he's sick for a day, and then he goes back to work. But this last one was bad, and he was very sick, worse than usual. Frances and I quarrelled. We fight all the time."

"Over Ewan?"

"Over my treatment of Ewan. Though never, I notice," she added bitterly, "over his treatment of me."

"And she's taken him to Switzerland? Why?"

She pushed herself off him, and stood up, and began ineffectually straightening her clothes.

"A rest cure. She thinks he's an alcoholic, and she's taken him to a clinic in Geneva, to see a specialist in the field. He won't see a doctor, and Frances thinks I should insist, or just bring one along, but it's so bad for him to be worried like that. Your mother used to do it at home, and it only made him worse out of spite."

"And is he alcoholic?"

She frowned. "Not really, not in the usual sense. He drinks for relief. There is nothing can prevent him drinking, unless he stops writing."

"What is he writing now?"

She came back to the piano and ran her hands along its top. "His fourth symphony."

His third had been finished here, at the villa, in the spring after that terrible Christmas; so it had been logical for Olivia to bring him back here to try to finish this new work.

"Hamil, it's so good!" Her face lit up. "It's the best thing he's ever written. Oh, I can't describe it. Maybe you can get some idea from the manuscript. I'll find you some later – he lets me touch it, though he won't let Frances, which makes her mad. It's a symphony with voices – two trebles and two counter-tenors, and a single soprano."

"That will be hard to put on," Hamil commented. "Full orchestra? I wonder if there are two counter-tenors in the world with voices strong enough to sing with an orchestra – let alone trebles."

"It doesn't matter if it gets performed or not," she said quickly. "I thought at first that performance was the important thing, but I can see now the truth of what Ewan tells me." Her excitement at the thought of the work was so great that she could hardly stand still. She lifted her head as if she might start dancing, and said, "He's written me into it. The soprano part's for me. Of course, my voice isn't equal to it – I'm only a church singer at best – but he has me in to sing the parts even so. And he says he writes for me; you know, *for me*, like a dedication."

"And yet," Hamil added carefully, "you implied a moment ago that he treats you badly."

The delight drained away. "Oh yes," she said flatly, walking to the door and staring out at the heat-hazed garden. Hamil had lost his sense of unreality, for as long as he was in this room with Livia he had his bearings, however unexpected their conversation might be. The world beyond the door, at which she stared unseeingly, was as unreal and irrelevant as the painted backcloth on a stage.

"Oh yes," she said. "That's the other Ewan. Ewan the musician is one thing, and Ewan the man is another." She turned to look at Hamil, her head radiating light from the sun outside. "I shouldn't speak of him contemptuously to you, of course, but – well, I call him *man*, but at times—"

"You can talk of anything to me, anything at all," he said. He desperately wanted her confidence, and he remained where he was, sitting very still, as if he feared any movement might startle her away. "Was that why you were crying?"

"It was one of the contributory factors," she said, and the irony in her voice was intended to conceal how deeply she felt. "Oh Hamil, these last few months have been desperate. He hurts me so much—"

Hamil closed his hands on his knees. He modulated his voice carefully.

"If he can hurt you, you must love him. He couldn't hurt you if you didn't love him."

If she were to say it, it would be like death to him, yet he put the words there in her way, deliberately. She walked back towards him, and her voice was normal, explanatory.

"No, no, you're wrong. I don't love him in that way, not in that way. But he loves me, you see, that's why he can hurt me. Of course, I care about him; I care what happens to him. I don't think you can be married to a person and not care about them. I mean, you must care about Irene, mustn't you? But I don't love him. I love you."

"Do you, Livia?"

She looked surprised. "Of course. Of course – oh, Hamil, you must know that."

"How could I know it? You married my brother."

"But that has nothing to do with it. You married Irene. What has marriage to do with it? You *must* know that I love you. After all we've done together—"

"All!" Hamil shook his head. "We have been together so little. We have—"

"I was thinking of quality, not quantity. A day with you is worth a year with anyone else in the world. Don't you think so?" He drew breath to answer, but she didn't wait for it. "Why did you come here?" she pointed out. "Not for Ewan."

"No. Not for Ewan."

As if that point were settled to everyone's satisfaction, she turned away again. He would have liked to stay on that subject, but perhaps it was too much to expect, given her state of suffering. "Ewan!" she said. "There is so much in him, so much talent, and evil. He is so *cruel*, Hamil. How he hurts me! He knows how – he discovers things about people. He's quick; he has a great insight. He knows the places he can wound me, and every time he does it I think he has gone beyond the point of all bearing. Yet I endure."

"But why? Why does he hurt you? I don't understand how he could. You said – you said he loves you."

"He loves me – yes, my mind, or my spirit, or whatever you call it. But he – hates – my body. He hates me." She grew tense, thinking of it, and her voice sank. "How he hates me. You know, don't you, that he is homosexual?"

Hamil was silent. He hadn't known it, but now she said it, it was not a surprise. It seemed to explain a number of things. "That Christmas," he said slowly, "when he ran away—?"

"Yes, it was to those people – the bad lot. It's not love between them, you know – I could bear that. They don't do the things they do because they love each other, or even because it gives them pleasure. They do them *because* they are bad. It gives them a thrill – but of course the thrill loses its edge with repetition, so they have to do more and more horrible and vicious things to get the same effect. Things an ordinary person would never be able to imagine."

She looked to see if he was following her and he nodded sparely, not wanting to think what those things might be, hating the probable fact that *she* knew what they were.

She went on. "If he loved a man and that helped him write, I could bear it – I'd welcome it. But they introduced him to drugs and vice, and now he can't do without them. He used to say they were the only people who understood him, and I scoffed at that. I thought he was only petting himself up, trying to make himself obscure. But he was right. That's why he ran away to them. I couldn't meet them again, but I had a long talk with them – just the once. And they do understand him, Hamil! Better than me, better than I ever could."

"Then why did he want you? He did, from the first time I ever saw you. He was always at your skirts, grabbing, demanding." He was angry at the memory. "He followed you around, interrupted your conversation, monopolised your company. And you let him – like an indulgent mother."

"Oh God, I don't know," she said. She sat down in the darkest part of the room as if she were exhausted, and he had to screw up his eyes to see her. "I suppose there was something in me he needed. I'm sure even he doesn't know what it is. You know how sometimes your body can demand things it needs without you knowing it – like pregnant women eating coal?" He nodded. "Perhaps it was like that with Ewan."

"But why did *you*—?"

"Because of the *music*!" She sat up, tensing herself again with the effort to make him understand the obvious. "*You* know! Your family have always put everything second to the creation of music – well, all art forms, but especially music. You've all spoilt Ewan, because he was brilliant."

Hamil shrugged. "Yes, I know we did, but I don't say it was the right thing to do. Is it so important after all?"

"Oh yes. What else lasts? Only music. Even love dies with us. Only the spirit that's in it – the fact of having created—" She turned her hands palm upwards on her lap and stared at them as if she were talking to herself rather than to him. "Even if the end product is lost, it has existed, and that's enough – almost enough. Only, I'm so tired."

A silence followed, in which Hamil considered the impossibility of crossing the length of the room that separated them. Then she began again, in a new voice, a sociable voice.

"So what are you doing here, all alone and unexpected?"

"You've changed," he said. "Years ago you wouldn't have asked me why I was here. You'd have said, 'You have to be somewhere,' and left it at that."

"You've changed too. Years ago you wouldn't have said that. You'd have thought it, maybe. You've so much more confidence now."

Astonishment deprived him of an answer for a moment. "Confidence? I was always brimful of confidence. That was my trouble as a young man – too much bloody confidence."

"I know all that, but all the same, you never got what you wanted, did you? Only other people's idea of what you ought to want, and that wasn't the same thing at all."

He was about to refute that, but paused out of justice to consider, and realised how little of what satisfied him he had ever had.

"Anyway, you haven't answered me. What are you doing here?"

"Playing hookey." He explained the circumstances, and she made a soft, ludicrous whistling.

"You're going to be in trouble, boy. That's both of us with a row to look forward to in two weeks' time."

"Two weeks?"

"That's how long Frances and Ewan are going to be away." She paused, and they stared at each other in growing realisation of the significance. It had not occurred to him to wonder, until that moment, how long he would be staying here. It had not occurred to her to consider that the fortuitous meeting could not last. The occasion acquired a beginning and an end, and was both greater and less than they could have expected, or even hoped for.

"Two weeks," Hamil said wonderingly. "We have two weeks?"

She made a wry face. "And then what? Well, to hell with the world. They'll get us in the end, you know."

"I know. We just have to make it worth it."

He cooked dinner while she made herself beautiful.

"That's your function," he had joked, "to inspire the creation of art forms."

"Don't," she had said, hurt. "That sounds like your mother's fantasy. I don't want to think about that."

"You won't be able to help it," he had said reasonably, "but it shouldn't hurt you, not now, not for a little while. Go and make yourself beautiful."

"Don't you need to make *yourself* beautiful?"

"That's not my function. I want to look at you. Go on; don't waste time arguing." And at the reminder that time was the known quantity in their particular equation, she had gone.

Cooking was a thing he did rarely, but well. There was a well-stocked freezer, and ample supplies of fruit and eggs and vegetables and dry stores. They did not stint themselves here, he thought, and wondered if they cooked for themselves or had a local woman in. He found the wine too, and the supply of hard drink, and pondered over its quantity and variety. He tried to imagine Livia's life with Ewan, and failed. Perhaps, he thought, it was as well that it was featureless to him, for he had an idea he might one day come to know altogether too much about it.

They ate on the terrace, late. The sun, unnaturally swollen, was sinking in a sky like a bruise, black and purple and ruby, and the light was both violent and fading, an ambivalence that suited the illusory quality of Olivia's beauty. All traces of her grief had gone, and she was calm and bright and serene, so entirely detached from her past and future that he felt she had given over all the rest of her life to him.

The blood ran out of the sky and the lantern on the terrace brightened and gathered moths. Everything was extraordinary to him, but he was glad of it, for it seemed in some way comforting – it was irrelevant, it could be ignored, leaving him with Olivia as the one small and impregnable oasis of reality. He felt that he could never tire of looking at her. In the uncertain light her vague beauty came and went. With the fluctuations of the tilley lamp, the shadows ran softly, like water, into the hollows of her face, and dispersed again, forming and reforming her a hundred times, moulding all her expressions three-dimensionally. By that much she seemed more alive, more like to life: a sculpture as against a painting.

There was nothing perfunctory about her. He never feared to see her face set into lines of polite incomprehension, concealed boredom, or unconcealed disapproval. She gave the full weight of her mind to everything that passed between them, however trivial. She never held back from him, retreating into a veiled sanctum of womanhood, the way Irene did when he bested her in an argument or asked her something she didn't like. And, though Olivia ought to have been exhausted by such continuous emotional expense, she seemed instead revived, recharged by it.

It was what he had always wanted, he thought – someone to be absolutely *with*. Someone in whom he could take refuge from the patch of dark inside him. She seemed as though she might even be, in the end, someone who could get rid of the dark completely, though that thought was only in the background. For the moment he was content to enjoy her company, and feel himself gradually relax. He was at ease with her. The agonising desire for her had ebbed away, and that too was comfortable, for however much he wanted her, he knew that he must not want to desire her. She was his brother's wife, and out of reach.

They talked at random, but inevitably the conversation came round to Ewan: he was continually in her thoughts, and for Hamil he was the aspect of her that caused him pain. Again he wanted to know what in particular Ewan had seen in Olivia.

"I think at first," she said, "it was just that I seemed to present an alternative to him."

"To what? To home?"

"Yes, and to the rest of society as he saw it. He saw me take Frances away. We seemed to him to lead an enchanted life, doing what we liked, without retribution."

"People had said that of me before you came," Hamil said. "Why didn't I become his hero?"

"You were, to an extent. He talks a lot about you. But he couldn't be with you and actually see it working."

"But why does he treat you so badly? One would think he hated you."

"Sometimes he does. I force him back to reality. I drag him out of the comfortable world of alcohol and drugs and into the crushing, agonising world of creation. He resents it. Of course, Frances plays her part in it too, but he doesn't attach much importance to Frances. In the world where he lives there's only him and me and the struggle."

"Why do you make him do it?" Hamil asked.

"Because I think it's important."

"Important? Personally? Or do you mean objectively?"

"I don't know about the objective part," she said. "I'm not sure I'm the right person to judge the global importance of his work. It seems to me brilliant, but then I'm not a musician. But in any terms, I think his writing is more important than his mere survival. Frances, of course, thinks otherwise. But it so happens that I have the power, and she does not."

"How hard you sound," he said. She turned her face a little

towards him, and the liquid shadows ran down her cheeks and the yellow lamp lit her eyes deep and soft. Hard? No, that was not the word. If she were hard, she would not feel the shocks, and he saw that she felt them.

"How about you?" she said. "Tell me about you and Irene. Tell me how you came to marry her."

"She was pregnant."

"I know that, of course. But that's not what I asked, and you know it."

"All right; it was evasion, I suppose," he said. "There was no challenge there. And it was the expected thing. How often, I wonder, have I done the expected thing without realising it at the time?"

"Did she expect you to be unfaithful to her?"

"Why should you think I am?"

"You're havering again," she smiled. "Answer the question."

"I suppose she did, in a way," he admitted. "She must have known, mustn't she, what I was like?"

"So that makes it all right?"

"All right? In whose judgement?"

"In your own, of course." She was not to be trapped. "But you don't need to answer. I see it doesn't. I should think that you suffer from your own infidelity far more than she does. She at least expected to suffer."

He held her gaze for a moment, and then wavered. It was a relief, after all. "I didn't know what it would be like," he said. "She's there all the time at the back of my mind. You know how it is when you've a sore in your mouth? You keep going at it with the tip of your tongue, and the more it smarts, the more you do it. All the time I keep thinking of her. I can't tell you what it's like."

She was silent in his pause, sympathetically.

"Sometimes," he went on, "we'll be all right for days, weeks. She'll be happy and busy with her own things, I'll be working and coming home tired, just for a meal and a bath, and we'll talk a little, pleasantly, about nothing in particular. Just ordinary life.

And then, suddenly, one evening, out of nowhere, we'll be in the middle of a flaming row. We shout, and abuse each other, and every nasty thing either of us has ever said or done will be dragged up and thrown. We're so unscrupulous – nothing is too mean for us."

Livia nodded, as if she understood.

"Then, when we've hurt each other as much as possible, it breaks off. She rushes out in tears, and I stamp about the house cursing. And later, much later, we meet again, and we're ashamed." He drank some wine. "So we're polite – that awful careful politeness, stepping round each other. I remember my parents being polite to each other like that, and I never knew why. I do now."

Livia nodded again. Hamil reached out across the table for her hand, but when she gave it the contact was unexpected, and startled him into withdrawing it again.

"That goes on for days sometimes, each of us creeping round the house and being distantly, unbearably polite to each other. And then it fades, and each of us realises that the other didn't apologise. The resentment's buried, and all the old hurts, until the next row brings them out again, and nothing is ever resolved. We don't put things right. We just stand at a distance and fight."

He had reached out again, and this time took her hand. She stroked his comfortingly, and he stared at her.

"Was it like that for them?" he asked.

"Who? Like what?" she asked.

"For my parents – so bleak. As it is for me."

"I think so," she said. "They could never be honest with each other. People so rarely are. You and Irene never talk properly, do you? I suppose, like your parents, you never will."

He still stared at her, as if she might make things come right for the world. She offered him a crumb of comfort.

"Do you remember I once said that your parents knew how far they could go? That they had found a working level? It seems to be that way. The dishonest relationships seem to be lasting.

Perhaps, if people were honest with each other all the time, it would become unbearable. An affair between people who were completely frank would probably be over very quickly."

"Do you believe that?" he asked.

"It doesn't matter," she said, understanding him. "The rule of majorities comes into action. It's quite impossible that all people, or even that most people, should be consistently honest. And we can't perpetually deal in hypotheses. 'If the horse of Troy had foaled, horses today would be cheaper to feed.'"

"Do you think," he asked cautiously, "that you and I are honest with each other?"

"More honest than we are with other people, at least. Don't you think so?"

"I think so. But I was afraid of the corollary," he said.

The days passed so easily that they seemed endless. Time stretched itself languorously to fit their lives, and the unvarying pattern of the weather and their pursuits made it hard to distinguish between the days. They rose early every morning and swam before breakfast while it was still cool, and then dried off on the terrace over a leisurely breakfast. The pleasure of being with Livia was so unremarkable that it was tempting to Hamil to think that, had they been married, life would have been like this always.

There *was* a woman, he found: a fat, handsome woman from the village who came in each morning to clean. It was she who brought their breakfast to them, along with the airmailed-in English papers, a fad of Ewan's. On the first morning he heard Livia explain his presence to Marisa in a limping sentence – she spoke little Spanish, only the few words she had learnt perforce since she had been here. Marisa rolled her eyes at Hamil, and it seemed doubtful that she had understood the explanation; or perhaps, having understood, she did not believe it. However, having rolled her eyes, she gave the ghost of a shrug which seemed to suggest she felt it none of her business anyway. Hamil spoke good French and German and fair Italian, but no Spanish, and Marisa spoke no language but her own. He smiled at her and she smiled back. It was enough that they should evince goodwill towards each other.

After breakfast they talked, sitting in the shade looking out on the unvaryingly blue sea. Sometimes Hamil practised, just to keep his lip in – the discipline of his life that was second nature to him. Sometimes, at Olivia's request, he played to her on the piano. They looked at Ewan's manuscript together, and he played some of it over as best he could. It was an extraordinary work, he thought – good in parts, certainly, but so unlike any of Ewan's earlier work that Hamil could make no judgement of its completed worth. It seemed fabulously complex, the scoring intricate, the virtuosity that would be required of the players outrageous, and he rather feared the attempt at understanding the mind that could have produced it. The more he looked at it, the more unlikely it seemed to him that it could ever be performed. The idea of using counter-tenors and trebles was brilliant, but were there any such voices in the world capable of sustaining these parts? Presumably the trebles would be boys. Or would it be possible to rescore the vocal parts for other voices – say sopranos and baritones? But would not that be to lose an essential quality?

The subject of the work was the love of two soldiers in the great Siege of Athens, a veteran and a boy. The soprano part was the narrator – a sort of solo Greek chorus, Olivia called it. It seemed strange to Hamil that Ewan should have said that he had written the soprano part for her. Did he see her as the classical "I" character – the wise watcher-from-outside, Shakespeare's Fool?

Though it had been scored for four male voices, there were only two characters: the doubling-up seemed to be for purely practical purposes. The vocal parts fascinated Hamil – he felt that there was great depth of feeling in them, but taking the piece purely as music, he had his doubts. He thought it would be too hard to listen to the piece for it ever to receive popular acclaim. And how would Ewan feel if his work should never come to performance? It was all right for Livia to say that was not important – she was not a musician.

Ewan's manuscript gave Hamil plenty to think about during the hot hours of the day when, after their light luncheon, they would retire to their separate rooms and lie dozing on their beds under the nets. And thinking about the manuscript brought his mind inevitably back to Olivia. Outside, the afternoon heat was relentless: damp, faintly unpleasant and panting beyond the louvred shutters, like a gigantic dog lying up against the house, immovable. Sleep at those times was impossible for Hamil. He would move restlessly, seeking relief even from the single sheet sticking to the sweating surfaces of his naked body; and his thoughts would run about like squirrels in a cage, carrying remembered sensations to the outposts of his body.

She was so close – only next door – also naked under a single sheet, perhaps thinking of him. Thinking in what way, though? She had been his lover once, but had married his brother. Did she desire him still? She had said she loved him, but did she, or did she regret what might now seem to her a rash impulse? If he could have been sure one way or the other, it might have been easier to bear the guilt of wanting her. She was his brother's wife: he came back always to that absolute.

And still he wanted her, and he loved her, and it was agonising. A part of his brain, less disciplined than the rest, told him to risk it. Risk being rebuffed? But when had he ever failed? Didn't he know the signs by now; hadn't he seen those signs in her expression and movements?

Risk being found out, then? But Livia wouldn't tell, even if she rebuffed him. Risk his own conscience – the worst taskmaster? But weren't his objections merely outworn conventions of society? Was there an absolute in this matter? Were there ever any absolutes?

Restlessly he would turn under the sheet and wonder if he

should leave. It might be best for both of them. He needn't necessarily go straight home; he could stay in a hotel for a day or two and finish his rest. Yes, that was best. That's what he would do. As soon as it cooled a little he would get up, pack, and go.

His decision made, he would doze more peacefully, Livia flickering in and out of his mind like a trout in a sunlit stream. And when at last he woke, and had showered and dressed, he would walk out on to the terrace, and Livia would join him, smiling her serene, loving smile. The cooling afternoon, the clear luminous evening would beckon with their easy delights, and he would relax into her company as naturally as a child waking. And he would not go. He was drowning painlessly in that stream, but he would not go.

Into this suspension of the Second Law, the weekend fell with an unexpected crash. Livia roused herself from her languor to explain that Marisa did not come in on a Saturday or Sunday, and that she usually drove into town on Saturdays to shop, and for a change of scene.

"If you like," she said, "we could have a meal out, just for a change. Unless," she added diffidently, "you'd rather stay here?"

"What on earth can you have to shop for?" he asked. "I thought this place ideally well found."

"Oh, odds and ends run out, and it's easier to get them all in one 'fowl swoop', as Frances says. And I like to look around the shops, and take coffee somewhere, and watch the people passing, and dine out. It refreshes me. I wasn't born to be a hermit."

Hamil laughed. "No one who had known you for any length of time could disagree with that. I'm only surprised you've stuck it out here for so long."

"What cannot be cured, as Nanny always said. Why does one attribute such banalities to nannies? I never even had a nanny."

"I did."

"Did you? Did you really?" This seemed to both surprise and amuse her. "How the other half lives," she added musingly. "Did you call her by her surname – Nanny Biggs? Like Noel Streatfield's children? Did she wear a cape and veil?"

"No to both. You *are* an ignorant."

"How could I know? I told you, I never had one."

"Dearest Olivia, I don't believe you even had a mother. You're an incubus. Or do I mean succubus? Whatever."

"Oh, I had a mother," she said airily. "Mothers are nothing to me. What I never had is a father – and now you know why I'm so fascinated by older men." She fluttered her eyelashes languidly, and he burst out laughing, aware that he had been diverted again, but no longer resenting it. One day, perhaps, she would tell him about herself.

They dressed more elaborately than they had for the past week, and Livia got the car – a smart white Triumph coupé – out of the garage. "It pays to drive an expensive car here – you get better service if they think you're rich." Hamil let her drive without even a protest – which would have amazed Irene had she been there – and relaxed beside her with his head back, watching the rich blue sky skim by overhead and listening to Olivia humming. He felt in holiday mood, and the mood persisted all through the day, a vivid contrast to the dreamlike state in which he had spent the previous week. All his senses were sharpened. His appetite was fresh too, and their lunch and coffee seemed to him almost Technicolor to the palate.

There was some kind of festival going on in the town, in honour of the local Virgin, and round every street corner they were likely to meet a group of tiny girls in large lace caps and long black skirts, shepherded along by larger versions of themselves carrying handbags. Olivia did her shopping in the manner of one eager to be sidetracked. She stopped to look in almost every shop window with catholic inclusion, and stared not only at displays but at passers-by with a frank curiosity that did not seem to offend in the least. On the contrary, it won her smiles and greetings, which she returned in her appalling sub-school Spanish.

Hamil was seized with the desire to buy her things; everything, in fact, for which she expressed any liking, however transitory. Having resisted it for some time, he finally broke down and found her charmingly happy to be bought for. She accepted a pair of sandals, in soft leather the colour and texture of pink marshmallow, with grave pleasure; and a silk scarf and a bottle of morello cherries and a leather belt with an elaborate brass buckle and a pair of thin silver hoops for her ears. Each thing she received with a separate and careful delight which seemed, somehow, of a piece with her expansive and careless joy in her surroundings and the day.

They looked around for somewhere to eat in the town, but saw nothing they liked.

"Do you like seafood?" she asked him at last. "Because if you do, there's a very good restaurant along the coast on our way back – we'd only need to go about a mile out of our way. And the view is magnificent."

"That would be lovely," he said. "We'll get there about sunset, won't we?"

"I should think so. It will be like eating at home, except that we'll be waited on."

By "home" she meant, of course the villa, and he realised as she said it how at home he now felt there. He had not realised the talent in himself for adjusting to surroundings and taking his shell with him. He had thought of himself as a man who needs a base, a security. Perhaps, he thought, he was more flexible than he had imagined.

The meal was excellent, and to please Livia, who said it was the cheapest good wine, they drank several bottles of the local champagne. Hamil, sturdy son of middle-class Edinburgh that he was, had rarely drunk champagne – only at weddings, his own included, and occasionally to please a girl – and then it had been cheap, sweet, and meagre. For the first time he was drinking as much as he wanted of a good champagne – even his untutored taste-buds could distinguish that it was good – and the name as much as the bubbles made him light-headed. It seemed to him outrageously extravagant to drink three bottles between them, and at once he felt transported to those young days in Edinburgh when Livia had lived on credit and eaten peaches and *foie gras* and skied with the Procurator Fiscal and two Dons and a Dean.

Heady days, when he was thin-skinned and hot-blooded and Livia had pursued in fact the kind of life for which he had been given credit by his seemlier contemporaries. "Do you remember drinking Black Velvet back in the flat in Thistle Street?" he asked.

Olivia smiled and joined in the game. The orange sun sank into a sea like thin grey silk; they had the small tiled balcony to themselves. "Do you remember watching the sun set at Aberlady?" she offered. "The most calm and beautiful night I ever remember."

"We'd been at North Berwick," he remembered. "We'd gone out to play golf, but it was too windy. You went for a donkey ride on the beach, and Frances stood watching you with envy sticking out all over her, but she was too dignified to try."

Livia laughed aloud. "Oh yes! But I never had any dignity. I hadn't time enough to spare for it – there was always so much to be done. We had tea in the Victoria Café to get out of the wind – do you remember?"

"No." He shook his head. "I don't remember that."

"Yes! Tea and those strange marshmallow things – Snowballs? And we played pinball on the flipper machine, and I told you we had a pinball championship at the university, and you didn't believe me."

"My God, yes, I remember now. Were you really so frivolous? I think it was your frivolity I loved. I was so bound up with acting my age, and you acted ten years younger and got away with it."

"Eighteen is the oldest age of all," Livia smiled. "I didn't say that, by the way – it's a quotation."

"Who from?"

"I forget." She shrugged. He shook his head, smiling. "But then the wind dropped, and we decided to walk part of the way home before catching the bus, and we walked to Aberlady, and then stopped because the sun was setting over the sands. The tide was right out, and the sand was smooth and shining, and the sea hardly marking it beyond, stretching out to the horizon so you couldn't tell where the sea ended and the sky began."

He remembered. "And how did that evening end?" he asked. "I know how it ought to have ended, but—"

She did not ask how. She looked at him, and he swallowed nervously. *I mustn't – I mustn't*, he told himself, but he didn't mean it, and knew he did not.

They spoke little after that. The silences stretched round them in thin, tight layers like plastic skins, and time and the surroundings grew more remote with each added layer. They listened to each other's breathing and the breath of the sea down below them, and counted the pulses of each minute and the flick of each eyelid's blink, waiting for the moment to build up enough common impulse to act without thinking.

Like swallows gathering on telegraph wires in autumn, the seconds added their individual weight, dropping singly from nowhere into the place where they were, slowly swelling into an impulse strong enough to move as one thought, direct, unhindered.

They seemed to have all the time in the world. It was quite dark, impenetrably dark when they reached home, and the air struck chilly off the sea.

"The wind's changed," she said, "It's the time of year – it often does at the end of summer. I'll light a fire."

There were pine logs in a basket, untouched since last winter. While she set about laying and lighting the fire, Hamil walked around easily, pouring drinks, touching and arranging things. One oblique lamp lit soft corners of things, leaving deep pockets of velvet shadow. The room was a haven, out of time, untouchable. What happened here was outside the normal rules of doubt and retribution. What happened here was immutable. He examined the presents he had bought her, pleased to have given them. The shopping was still packed in bags on the floor, and he remembered buying fresh peaches, and searched for them.

Livia was kneeling still in the hearth, and into the hooning quiet the logs were throwing sharp ticks of spark and flame. Hamil brought a tumbler of whisky across to her, and a peach the size of his hand, and a small knife. She looked up at him, and he knelt beside her.

"Don't move," he said. She sat on her heels, watching him, her eyes so still on him that they might have been apprehensive. He cut the stone out of the peach, and sliced the flesh, and fed it to her piece by piece. "Your hands will be dirty from the logs," he explained. He dipped the last slice of the fruit in the whisky, and fed that to her. "See, I have you feeding from my hand," he crooned. "What does it taste like?"

"Like peaches in whisky," she said. "Try some."

"It's all gone," he said. He drank some whisky and gave her some, and then put the glass down on the hearthstone. He must touch her now – he had waited long enough. He put his hands either side of her head and stroked her hair. "You should have some perfume – no! Don't get up. I'll get it. I want you to be perfect now."

"In my room," she said.

"Isn't there some in your handbag?" He didn't want to move so far away from her. The fire spurted and spat, but she didn't flinch away. She nodded. He fetched it – a tiny vial of Le Bois, almost all gone. He turned the bottle upside down on his palm and shook out enough to anoint her with, and as it touched her warm skin the thin green scent expanded and afforested the room. "Pine trees," he said. "Some green, some burning. It's like home." And by home, he meant Scotland.

She smiled happily and held out her arms, and the firelight ran off their rounded flanks like water. She turned them in the liquid light, lifting her palms to him.

"See," she said. "My hands aren't dirty at all." He leaned forward to her, and her hands reached him at last, touching his face, and his own hands completed the contact, sliding up her arms to her shoulders.

Water slips down imperceptibly to form a drop, and the drop grows heavier until the moment comes when it falls. A conclusion may arrive too in that manner, unspoken, between people who have no way of knowing each other's minds, and yet who act in that simple moment with such accord there can be no doubt, hesitation, or guilt. The action breeds itself out of the gathering moment, and it is done.

It was after that, during the long night and day in which they made love and talked with barely any distinction between the two kinds of action, that she told him about Ewan.

"It happened on that day we were talking of – when we went to North Berwick," she said. "In the evening, I don't know why, everyone went away. I think perhaps you had to work. I can't remember where Frances went, but Ewan and I were left alone. It was the kind of day that leaves an atmosphere behind it, rather like the airy, emptied-out feeling you have when you come home late after a day's hard exercise – hunting or sailing, perhaps.

"Ewan made something to eat for us – he was trying to learn to cook, and your mother wouldn't let him experiment at home. Then we sat on the floor and listened to some music. Brahms, I think. Frances and I were going through Brahms at the time. Like first love, one never quite gets over Brahms."

Hamil moved a little so that he could watch her face. "You really loved Frances, didn't you?" he said.

"Oh yes, of course. She was the first of you. She's changed, now, and I'm so sorry. But she was lovely then. And Ewan, so like her, like her twin. His lungs full of sea air and his mind full of music and atmosphere. Perhaps it wasn't really him at all. Perhaps he was just the representative.

"He trembled so – all over, like a string vibrating. I've never known anyone so excited, not ever in my life. It made me feel almost awed, as if he were more than himself. Horribly sacrilegious, I know, but it made me think of the immaculate conception."

She looked apologetic, and he smiled a little at this, despite his pain.

"Afterwards, he was sick. I think it was just too much for him. He jumped up, swaying as if he was dizzy, and then he stumbled out of the room and I heard him being sick in the bathroom. Poor Ewan."

She rolled over against Hamil and hid her face on his shoulder. From that position of safety she went on, her voice stronger from its hiding place.

"He never could again, you know, not in the ordinary way. He could only love men, physically. Afterwards, after we married, when he tried to do it, he just couldn't. At first he would cry, and I would pet him and say, 'Don't worry, it's all right.' How we say that, when it so obviously isn't! For weeks he worried about it, and I was understanding and kind and noble. And then – well, then, one day—"

Her voice had hardened, and instinctively he held her tighter, as if to protect her from what was coming.

"One day, he came home late, and drunk. He'd been out with his friends – the bad boys. I lay very still pretending to be asleep, because I didn't want to have to discuss his being drunk. I wasn't angry, but I knew that he'd expect me to be, and that he would behave exactly as if I'd picked a quarrel, whatever I said.

"I know so well the sound of him coming in drunk: the heavy breathing, the sound of clothes and shoes being dropped where they come off, the stumbles and curses when he bumps into something in the dark. Then the bed lurches as he puts his weight on it, and he clambers in."

She was trembling now, her body against his arm, her voice against his ear. "His skin is cold and a little clammy. He smells of drink – that awful, stale, beery smell of a drunken man – and cigarette smoke. For a minute he lies still, and I think he may drop off to sleep – and then he mutters something, and rolls over, and reaches for me—"

She stopped abruptly. He wanted to tell her not to go on, but he couldn't speak. Was this Ewan? Or some other man? Or all drunken men the world over who climb into bed beside their sleepless, miserable wives? Why do men do this to women? And why do women do this to men? Must they torture one another, each with their own weapons, of cruelty and, subtler, of suffering?

She went on, her voice a spike of pain on the quiet darkness. "He reached for me, and I kept very still, not daring to speak, hoping he might fall asleep. But he fondled me, and said, 'I ought to make love to you, since you're my wife. I'm not doing my duty by you, am I? But I can't make love to your face, can I? You know I can't do that. So I'll just have to make love to your back.'"

Hamil wanted desperately to stop her, but he couldn't speak, and only held her tighter, hoping she would understand. She paused a while, and when she resumed her voice was normal, conversational.

"Well, that's the way it was after that. He couldn't have normal sex with me, and I would gladly have left it at that, but he insisted. He tried out new things his *friends* taught him. He hates my body, and he's done everything he can to make me ashamed. He almost succeeded. And yet, he wants to love me. The struggle's always been apparent – in his music on the one hand, and in bed on the other. It's torn him apart, as it's torn me."

She drew back from Hamil, and sat up, her flanks and hanging breasts rosy in the low light from the fire. Her face was in darkness, but the dark was warm, and out of it her voice came, lifting gratefully. "That's what he's done, Hamil, he tried to make me ashamed – but you, you've given me back what he took from me. And I love you. I would have loved you anyway, but now – I have such a debt to repay."

He loved her, then, and through the night, and the next day; again and again and more and more, seeking her out whenever – out of fear, or greed of herself – she held back. He flushed her out of the coverts where she hid from him; where she retreated he followed; where she shrank back, flinching, he reached out and touched her again until, backed into the corner of his determination to give her pleasure, she yielded herself up, shuddering with terrible joy.

He had to eradicate Ewan's mistake, and then rebuild. It had been a mistake. She had been for one of them, and all of them had wanted her, but it was for Hamil to consummate the relationship. It was for him that the flower would open, and it had been a mistake that the wrong person had taken her. Gravely and joyfully he loved her, and in taking her final surrender, he gave himself up also for lost. Here, at last, was the private place he had known had existed, the safe, high-walled garden where nothing was blighted or died; where companionship and passion and love were the same thing, and there was no more loneliness. His soul fed on utter contentment, and it was impossible to be afraid – even of the knowledge that, once having lived here, he could never be happy anywhere else, ever again.

There was no Time here – but no Time, and no time, though the same thing, mean the opposite. The days passed. Wandering blissfully about the stunted, aromatic garden under the endlessly renewed sun, they knew that the moment was approaching rapidly when their brother and sister would come back, and the thing must end. Arms wrapped around each other they strolled, and spoke of it as a distant inevitability, but when the time came and it was the eve of the arrival there seemed no choice, no decision to be made.

"I had better not be here when they arrive," he said. He had seduced his brother's wife. Not only was that morally a crime, it was also, in canon law, incest. There could be no grace in him. There was nothing to be done about it – at least, not immediately. But to give up that high-walled garden for ever was equally impossible.

"What will you do?" he asked her.

"Do? What is there to do?"

"But you can't stay with him for the rest of your life, like this; you can't go on like this."

"No," she said, "Not for ever. Perhaps only for a little while longer, but at least you must see that he has to finish this work, and that I am in some way essential for that."

"Well, if you say so – but afterwards?"

"I think things will be different afterwards. He won't need me. He is, in any case, very ill. I don't think he will live to a great age. Others may replace me as nurses."

"And then – you'll come to me?"

"But what will you do? What about Irene and your children? No, Hamil, you see there's nothing we can do."

"We'll find a way," he said. How strange that in the crises of one's life, one spoke in clichés. "There must be something we can do. It can't just end like this."

"Oh, it won't end," she said comfortingly. "How could it? But we may not be able to be together very much."

They slept together for the last time, and in the morning she woke him early, so that he would be able to get away before Frances and Ewan came home. But as he rose from the bed she held out her arms to him, helplessly, like one drowning, and he went back to her. He might, having steeled his mind, have managed to tear himself away, but in the last moment it was she who could not let him go.

Eight

And so it was that he was there when Ewan came home. All the emotions he expected to feel were swept away in the first minutes by his shock at how his brother had declined. He felt resentful towards Livia that she had not prepared him more thoroughly for the shock; and yet he had to realise that he could not have expected this, even had she told him.

Frances helped him from the car like a nurse with an elderly invalid. His sister, too, had changed, grown suddenly middle-aged before her time – flat-shoed, ungainly, careless of her own looks or her share of the attention. She seemed at first more of a wife to Ewan than Livia was, fussing round him and supporting his elbow up the step to the patio. Yet it was to Livia that his eyes went, and though his greeting for her was a diffident, "Hello," unaccompanied by touch or kiss, Hamil could feel something of the power that had pulled his brother back.

"It's good to be home," Ewan said, settling himself slowly in an armchair and easing his legs out straight as if they hurt him. *Gouty*, Hamil's mind suggested irrepressibly, and he was faintly shocked at himself.

"Do you regard this as home?" Hamil asked.

Ewan shrugged indifferently, but his eyes went to Livia, quiet and careful on an upright chair across the room. "I've made it my home," he said.

Frances came in from the kitchen with fruit juice in a jug, and glasses. She glanced, too, at Livia, and her expression hardened.

"You might give a hand," she said sourly.

Olivia looked at her, but there was no trace in her face of the love she had once borne for the younger woman.

"You seem to be managing magnificently. I'm sure I should only be in the way."

"Oh, she feels neglected, don't you, Fanny? You make her feel so dowdy, with your fashion and your make-up."

"There's no sense in tarting myself up when I'm all day nursemaiding you," Frances retorted, turning her hard look on Ewan, who smiled maliciously.

"Yes, of course, that's what you put me in mind of," he said with a sudden burst of inspiration. "A jailor. That's what you are, ain't you, Fan? A hard-faced old bitch of a wardress."

"Oh, stop it," Frances snapped at him. "You're not amusing."

"Oddly enough," he replied, "neither are you."

"I'm not here to amuse you. I'm just here to do the work," Frances said.

Despite her sharp words, she was pouring the drinks and handing them round. Hamil took his, and watched Livia receive her glass and stare down at it as if it might contain a viper. She looked up at him, her gaze scalding him for a moment, and then away. *You see*, she seemed to be saying, *what it's like*.

"And Livy's just here to look nice," Ewan said. His unpleasant smile wavered a little as it turned on Livia, and Hamil felt that all the foregoing exchanges had been a warming-up for his encounter with her.

"Come here," he said. It sounded like a command, and Olivia got up and walked across the room to him, not quickly, but not with any visible reluctance. As soon as she was within reach he grabbed at her and pulled her down on to his lap. She half fell, overbalancing, and yet it was he that looked clumsy, not her.

Ewan pushed his face into the cleft of her bosom, nuzzling, while his arms went round her and squeezed. Livia bore with his caresses blankly, her eyes nowhere, but Hamil could not bear to see that sickly face and body so close to her. He looked away pointedly, looked at Frances, and saw that she stared at the couple with hot anger.

"You might encourage me a little – mightn't she, Fan?" Ewan exclaimed suddenly, petulantly, lifting his head away. Where it had been there was a red mark on Livia's flesh. "After all, you are my wife – my *wife*, you know."

"Don't bring me into it," Frances began. "You should keep that sort of thing for when you're alone."

"But she doesn't let me when we're alone," Ewan said maliciously. "Well, not often anyway – though there are times, aren't there, my darling wife? Times when—"

"Stop it!" Hamil said, rising to his feet in disgust and rage. "I've had enough of this. For God's sake, what's the matter with you?"

"Hasn't she told you?" Ewan said. "I'd have thought she'd have given you all the details by now."

Livia said quietly, "Don't interfere, Hamil."

"*Has* he been interfering, wife?" Ewan asked her pointedly.

She turned and looked at him at last, and then abruptly leaned her face down to his. For a moment Hamil thought she meant to kiss him, but then saw that she only whispered something. Ewan's face went white. Pale though he was, Hamil saw the change of colour even across the room, and Ewan stood up abruptly, shaking Livia off his lap.

"I need a drink," he said harshly, and went from the room. There seemed a blessed silence in his wake, which Frances broke at last.

"You always have to do it," she said bitterly. "You set him off deliberately. He's been all right for two weeks – two whole weeks – and now see what you've done."

Livia had been standing where Ewan left her, looking dazed. "You call that all right?" she said. Her voice was still carefully neutral.

"You know what I mean," Frances said. Hamil, looking at her, felt suddenly that she had blurred – her face, her figure, her voice, her mind. She seemed so worn and rubbed away that even her ineffectual, wool-gathering youth seemed by comparison to have been sharply focused normality.

"Yes, I know what you mean. You mean sober. He has been sober – but has he done any work?"

"Work, work, that's all you care about. You don't mind what happens to him, so long as he writes, even if it means he has to be perpetually drunk."

"Yes, that is all I care about," Livia said. She was still calm, but her voice had taken on an edge. "What is he worth unless he writes? All he is is his music, and anyone who tries to kill that kills him."

"Yes, that's what you'd like, isn't it, to kill him? You have no humanity."

"Is *that* humanity?" Livia said, and gestured angrily towards the door through which Ewan had just passed. "There's no intrinsic merit in being alive – the least of the insects does as much. What use is he to anyone as he is?"

"He doesn't have to be any use," Frances cried passionately. "He's my brother, for God's sake."

"Don't bring your God into it! Ewan is a composer, and I won't let you stop him writing."

"Even if it means letting him die?"

"They would shoot a dog that suffered as much," Livia said. "Frances, listen," she began again, and Hamil, whose eyes had not left her, saw the kindness in her face, the last residue of warmth left from their girlhood together. But Frances was not looking; she was wiping the tears of anger and hurt from her eyes, and she turned away her face stubbornly.

"No, I don't want to listen. You can twist anything to make it sound right. You wormed your way into our family, and now you're breaking it apart. All right, so Ewan's your husband, but he's our brother! He's more ours than yours." Hamil realised, awkwardly, that he was being included in that "we", that Frances was ranging herself at his side against Livia. He glanced at his sister fearfully.

Livia gave a small, tired smile. "We are what we are," she said. "All of us, to make what we can of ourselves and leave behind the best—"

"I won't let you kill him," Frances interrupted. She glared at Livia, and Livia looked back steadily. She seemed reluctant to go on, and Hamil at last added his own weight.

"Need you push him? After all—" Impossible to say what he wanted to say. *After all, you needn't be his wife*. Livia knew, of course, what was in his mind, as she knew what was in Frances's, and in Ewan's. She was the only one who knew all the cards.

"You can ask him, if you like. But I know what he would say. It's me he wants." She looked from one to the other. "Ask him! But he knows my way is right."

The moment endured, and Hamil thought that Frances must be convinced. But with an abrupt, characteristically graceless movement, she turned away and went to the door into the kitchen, feeling outward for it with her hand as if she were blinded with tears. But her eyes were dry when she turned again at the door to speak.

"There's no room for me here, I can see that." She pushed open the door and then turned again as another thought struck her. "I'll never speak to you again."

The door fell to silently after her, and Livia sighed, crumpling a little. "Christ," she said softly. "What a family. *He's* in the study drinking, and *she's* in the kitchen crying." She paused. "You don't approve, do you?"

"Approve?"

"Of me. Of the way I handle things."

"I don't think it's a matter of approving," he said awkwardly. "I could wish you had never met any of them."

"Except you?" she said wryly.

"Naturally, except me. But would that have been any good? You wouldn't even have looked at me if I hadn't been Frances's brother." His voice sounded bitter when it reached the air, and he was sorry. He hadn't meant to let old jealousy show through.

Livia sighed again. "Oh Hamil, I can't be to blame for everything," she said. "I don't think they would have been much different anyhow. She always nursed him, even when I first knew them. They – compensate for each other."

"But what's wrong with him?" he burst out passionately. He couldn't quite forget the younger brother he had taught to play football. Ewan was eight years younger than him, and looked ten years older.

"It's nothing obscure," she said. "He just can't face up to life. Some people have nervous breakdowns, some commit suicide, others hide in various ways—"

"Oh, that's all—" He waved a hand dismissively. "All that psychological shit. He was spoilt as a child, I suppose. But why is he so sick-looking? Is he ill? It can't all be drink. Christ, I drink. You drink. You drink more than me."

"If you mean his physical condition, it's a mixture of many things," she said. "Drink and drugs and other abuses of his immune system. He doesn't eat properly. All his organs are gradually breaking down. His liver's affected. He has ulcers. Colitis. Infections. But that's only his body. Why do you put so much importance on the body?"

"What do you mean, why? Don't be stupid." He hated this sort of talk, which emphasised to him how far he had fallen from grace, from his youthful idealism.

"You know what's important. The body is – nothing at all."

"If I could, right now, I would show you it's important. I'd make you admit it," he said in a low voice.

Now she looked at him, her eyes leaping into him with the intimacy of shared lives, far more than they had ever really deserved.

"Don't talk about making me," she said. "You gave me back my body, which he took from me. Don't spoil that gift."

He could not answer. The intimacy ebbed, and there was a

spark of cynicism in her eyes as she said, "Besides, as Ewan would no doubt tell you, I am his wife. That much I owe to all of you. And he makes good use of me."

The next day Ewan was ill, feverish and nauseous. He had the shakes, he evacuated constantly, his face was yellow and shiny with sweat.

"Drink," Livia said to Ewan briefly as she left him for a time to Frances. They took turns at sitting with him, but Frances, true to her word, had not spoken to Livia. "It brings him on this way. He'll be better tomorrow. Frances was a fool to let him dry out."

"Don't you *care*?" Hamil asked, forced despite himself to pity his brother. Ewan was a disgusting but heart-rending sight.

"Would I be here if I didn't?" Livia asked shortly. "I don't like to see him suffer like that. He wouldn't if Frances didn't dry him out."

"Or if, when she had dried him out, he didn't drink again."

"Nothing in the world will stop him drinking," she said. "It's all that keeps him alive."

"It will kill him," Hamil protested.

"That too," she agreed. And then her face crumpled. "Oh God, oh God, I wish you would all leave me alone. You've got your roots in my heart, and you're eating away at me."

She left him abruptly.

The next day Ewan was better, out of bed.

"It's that wonder brew of Livy's," he said cheerfully. "It stops up my bum like a rubber bung." He was sitting in the kitchen eating breakfast, haggard but chirpy. "It tastes like the wrath of God, but it does the trick."

"You should eat more," Frances said, unable to allow Livia the credit. "It's drinking on a empty stomach that brings this on. Even if you only take a glass of milk, that would be better than nothing – but you should never let your stomach get empty."

"I'll take my brandy in a glass of milk, for you, my darling little sister," he said. "It's ma tubes, doctor, it's ma tubes. What did we ever do to deserve being cursed wi' a wame fu' o' tripes?"

"How about a swim after breakfast?" Hamil suggested tentatively. He wanted above all to preserve the miraculous good temper Ewan seemed to have found for himself.

"Can't be done, old boy," he said. "I must go in and work. Can't you see my muse behind my chair, with a stop-watch? Time and motioning me. I can't afford to mess around like you salaried musicians. And by the way, aren't you supposed to be somewhere?"

There seemed an edge to the question. "Tomorrow," Hamil said shortly. His life beyond this place seemed both threatening and unsubstantial, and he did not know how that could be.

"'Tomorrow and tomorrow and tomorrow, creeps in this petty pace from noon to noon,'" Ewan quoted. "'To the last syllable of recorded time.' To the last syllable and the full stop. It's the full stop one minds so dreadfully." And he looked round for Livia suddenly, as if frightened. "Ain't it, Livy?" he appealed.

"It's only shadows," she said, surprisingly kindly. "Strong light always throws shadows."

Hamil didn't understand what she meant, but Ewan seemed to. He said, cheerful again, "Yes, and I must go and stoke mine up, mustn't I? 'Lead, kindly Light.' Shakespeare and Cardinal Newman – erudite today, aren't we? If you'll excuse me."

He left an unhappy silence behind him, in which Frances glared at Livia and once or twice seemed on the verge of breaking her resolve. Livia ignored her and asked Hamil, "Are you really going tomorrow?"

"Yes," he said. He wanted to ask, "Do you mind?" but couldn't, not with Frances there.

"I wish you weren't," Frances said suddenly. "We'll miss you."

"Sort of buffer state?" he asked.

"*I'll* miss you," she said. "I don't see enough of you – any of you," she added, meaning the family. "Only poor Ewan."

"The exiles," Hamil said. "Mother has a lot to answer for, sending you here."

"No," Frances said quickly, defensively. "It's better this way – she's right. But it's hard on me."

"And Livia," he prompted, but Frances only looked down at her plate unhappily.

"I just wish you weren't going."

"I'll come back if I can," he said.

"Don't leave it too long," Frances said. "Or you may be too late."

She got up hurriedly, knocking over her chair, and ran out on to the patio. Hamil made to follow her, but Livia stopped him. "It's all right. Leave her to cry for a minute. I'll go out to her in a minute."

"You?"

"It's what she wants," she said, and he didn't know if she meant the crying, or Livia herself.

That night – very late, for Ewan had been up working until almost two – Hamil left the bed that had seen so little of him and sought Livia's.

The moonlight streaming in from her uncurtained window lay across the middle of her bed, illuminating the one white arm that lay outside the sheet, though her face was in darkness, as he must have been to her.

Her net was not down. She had been expecting someone. "I knew you'd come," she said softly out of the dark.

"How did you know who it was?" he asked.

He pulled the sheet off and crouched over her. He thought for one searing moment of her being in bed with Ewan. He wished he didn't know about that. She shouldn't have told him about that: now he could never un-know it. He felt all his frustrated anger at the situation rising up in him, rising as irresistibly as his desire rose at her mere closeness. She should not have this power, and not be touched by it herself.

But she said, "How could I not know you?" And she held up her arms, supplicating. They rose white out of the surrounding dark, as if she were Helle drowning in the black water. "Love me," she begged.

You can't separate love and loving, she had said. Warm in me, a living presence – wasn't that blasphemy? Yet how could this completeness be blasphemous? He pressed down into her, and forgot self as the holy are said to forget self in contemplation. They moved together, easily, like swimmers, held in the dear moment, lips touching, breathing each other's breath. For the long, for the infinite moment of approaching coitus he was no longer lonely or alone. "Come in me, be in me," she whispered. She belonged to him. He shuddered and yielded himself up.

They turned like swimmers, parting only to lie more comfortably, her head on his shoulder, his cheek resting against her hair. He loved her now, at this moment, with a vast, strange tenderness that he would not have expected, a feeling he imagined a mother might feel towards her infant. He loved her warmly, as if she was part of him. Now, on the edge of parting from her, he wanted to say, "Take care of yourself, be happy" – all manner of useless things that were really only endearments. *My dear, dearest, my darling – not my anything, of course, but still, to me, dear.*

The moon had moved round and the bed on which they lay was in darkness. If he did not leave now they would both fall asleep, and it would not do for them to be discovered sleeping together in the morning.

"I wish I could sleep with you," he said, breaking the silence at last. "I wish I had the right to sleep with you."

It seemed her thoughts had kept pace with his through that long silence. "Stay with me," she said. "I'll wake you in time."

So he stayed, trusting her.

Nine

March 1975

The train, with its passive clamour, made him feel restless. He crossed and recrossed his legs, and Irene, on the other side of the carriage, looked up at him reprovingly. Her glance said, as clearly as words, *Don't set a bad example to the children.* He tried to keep still – truly, the boys were being very good at the moment, their identical fair heads bent over identically banal comics.

"I only seem to go home now for funerals," he said apologetically. Irene looked up from *Woman's Own* and down again. She did not say, "Don't exaggerate," but then she didn't have to. The things for which she chided him were a well-regulated body, a fine upstanding army of persistent faults. *I've told you a million times not to exaggerate.*

Sorry, ma'am. All right, so this is only the second funeral I've been home for. But pray tell me, when else have I been home? And how many funerals do you *call a lot?*

The ranks are thinning, he thought. He remembered, inevitably, the last time he had travelled north to a family funeral. By car, that time, and alone. Irene had not wanted to travel so far with the children so young. "They'd be in the way, and the atmosphere would upset them," she had said. So this time they were supposed to have fun? *A barrel of laughs, my family – the bastards keep dropping dead.* Exaggeration again – only once each.

"Children need the experience of death, as of anything else," Irene had pronounced this time. She was using up her slack reading child psychology and joining parent-teacher associations. It made her dangerous to live with. Women shouldn't have theories, he generalised recklessly. They work best off impulse drive. But the upshot was that Irene, with a theory, had it all ways over Hamil with none, and the children were to go up for the funeral – the service anyway, if not the stronger meat of the graveside.

"Don't they need the experience of that?" Hamil had asked – a little crudely, perhaps, but he had gone beyond the stage of bayoneting Irene – these days he resorted to blunt instruments.

"Enough, Hamil, is enough," she had replied, leaving him to wonder what to apply the remark to.

Going by train was both an advantage and a disadvantage. It was less tiring not to drive, but the inaction made him restless and irritable and, though being on the train meant he could drink if he wanted, he knew Irene didn't like him to drink when they were out with the children. One thing cancelled out another and left him suspended in limbo.

Limbo – what a word! His Aunt Hannah had once had a budgerigar called Bimbo. Aunt Hannah, the godmother of himself and Frances, had taken a close interest in their education and upbringing. He remembered how once, when she had gone to France for a holiday, she had left him and Frances to look after Bimbo, feeling that it would be a valuable experience for them. She and Irene were sisters in spirit.

The bird had been brought round in a covered cage just as they – the children – were going to bed, so they had not been allowed to look at it until the next morning. When they did, creeping through the house in the icy dawn for the purpose, their disappointment had been shattering. Bimbo was without doubt the most disgusting creature Hamil had encountered. Originally green, he was now a piebald pink where he had scratched his feathers out; his appearance vied with a nasty nature to make him the number one undesirable of the bird world.

Frances, in her long flannelette nightgown, with her fuzzy hair in two bunches, had stared in a mixture of pity and disgust at the scabrous creature leering at them from behind his bars. Hamil, in striped pyjamas, hopping from foot to foot because he had forgotten his slippers and the parquet was icy, had no pity.

"No wonder they kept it covered," he had said. "She must be potty to keep the thing. It ought to be squirted with something – isn't there such a thing as budgie-spray?"

"Don't be cruel, Hamil," Frances had protested, but she had giggled all the same.

The evil old bird had outlived Aunt Hannah – she was in fact his great-aunt, and suitably aged – and Aunt Hannah, in a spirit of indestructible cynicism, had left the bird in her will to Hamil. Hamil had given it to Nanny to look after in her retirement bungalow at Silverknowes. Nanny's Christian spirit had been equal even to that.

"Marvellous woman, Nanny," he said aloud, and this time all three of them looked up, and he felt foolish and tried to look unconcerned and whistle. Nanny had been at Ewan's funeral – perhaps the only person there whose love and grief were unclouded by memory, for Nanny had never known how Ewan turned out. To her he was still the baby, the talented one, cut down in his prime, like the flowers of the forest, and all the young soldiers who went off to war in 1914. Hamil remembered how, bent and half blind, but still coherent in her mind, Nanny had clutched Livia's arm and said, "After all, I'm glad he had you, dear, even for that little time." Nanny, knowing nothing, had perhaps known best.

And Olivia – what had she felt? She had spoken kindly to Nanny, and looked after her at the gathering afterwards, making sure she had sherry and cake enough, and someone to talk to. A monument, that was what Nanny had called her: a monument of calm. Yet she had looked – Hamil tried to recall her face, but though the details presented themselves readily enough, he could not assemble them into any wholeness or reality. Heavily pregnant; her face white as wax and her eyes strained and shadowed, though whether with Ewan's death or his foregoing illness Hamil did not know. Black clothes, white face, yellow hair. Eyes full and burning. Mouth set. He remembered, and didn't remember.

There had been so much to think about, so much to worry about. Livia – the baby: his? Surely his. But, oh my God, possibly, just possibly Ewan's? There had never been a moment when he could talk to her about it. And had Ewan suspected what had taken place between them? And how did she feel now?

Ewan's illness – his last and best work – if it was his best. The task laid upon Hamil by the dying Ewan to have his last work edited, published and performed: was it good enough? Was he good enough?

A memory in photograph form, of Livia supporting his mother. His mother had taken it badly, worse than any of them. Of all of them, she had loved Ewan best, needed him the most. She had needed his brilliance, his success; needed possession of him, through her own power and through Livia's body. Had she suspected the affair between Livia and Hamil, it would have killed her. And now she clung to Olivia – called her dear Livia, using the abbreviation she had always scorned – and greedily talked about her baby. Mother hunger, the hunger for a baby in the house – Hamil had read of it often enough, but this was more; it was Ewan's baby she wanted. It was some kind of monstrous consummation, the one she had sought for years through their father, and had never achieved.

And Livia – strangely, after all that had happened – had been kind to her, supported her and attended to her much as she did to Nanny, but with a sympathy that Hamil, in his extended state, could feel even from a distance.

There had been little time to talk to Livia on The Day, or even the day afterwards, with so much to do, so many relatives around, so many people staring at her and oohing and aahing with pity for the young pregnant widow. But later they had spent some time together, ostensibly to read over the will. Hamil had not been able to get away for the official reading, being heavily engaged at the time, and there was a paragraph that concerned him.

"You had better use my study," Father had said when he overheard the subject mentioned. "You'll want to be alone with no interruptions, and that's about the only place in Edinburgh that can guarantee that."

He was right – Father's study had retained a kind of holy inviolability through all the changes in the family's life. But had he offered it for any deeper reason? Certainly he had looked at them significantly, but then all Father's actions and words were so slow and dignified they took on a weight and significance they perhaps might not have deserved.

Thinking of his father now, Hamil felt the tears springing to his eyes, and he had to close them to disguise the fact. He leaned his head back and pretended to sleep while he tried to relax the tears away. He could not yet accept the idea of his father dying. Though Ewan's death had moved him, he had not cried, but for his father the tears sprang readily. Father's whole life seemed to have been so bleak and unhappy – a marriage that gave him no comfort, children who did not understand him. He had been a withdrawn, detached, cynical, sad man, whose life Hamil might hold up for himself as the example of what should not happen to the worst of men – and his father had not been the worst of men.

And that day had revealed again, so Hamil thought, the strange sympathy he had with Livia. Mr Strathearn had never been a demonstrative man. He was not even a loving man. Hamil, who loved him, would have liked to suppose he loved his children underneath that dark, detached manner – but he could not be sure of it. Yet that day, as on other occasions, Hamil had felt the affinity between his father and Livia. He had wished so often that his father could have loved him. Yet it was a comfort to know that there was a possibility he had loved someone: if he loved anyone, he loved Olivia.

And in his father's study, amongst the neglected books, he and Livia had had their one private talk. They had, in fairness, gone through the business first, reading through the paragraph of the will in which Ewan, with touching trust, had made Hamil his musical executor.

"He really thought me capable of it?" Hamil had said in wonder.

"Ewan knew how good a musician you are," Livia said, with her usual exactness meaning both how good and how bad. "What is more surprising is that he should have supposed you'd fulfil the trust."

Hamil was hurt. "Am I so unreliable?"

"I mean," she said, "that he knew you wished you had married me. And knowing that, it made it rather pitiful and strange that he should have given you such power over him. And yet—" She paused reflectively. "He knew he was dying, of course, and when people are dying they naturally assume everyone has forgiven them everything, and all is sweetness and light. Everyone is a Dora at a moment like that."

"A Dora?"

"*David Copperfield*," she supplied absently.

He wanted her to go on talking, but couldn't think of any way to prompt her. At last he asked, awkwardly, "How was it? I mean – you didn't suffer too much, did you?"

She lifted her face to him, and he saw that it was marked with sorrow, but that she was not overcome. She absorbed shocks. "I was attached to him, Hamil, whatever happened. He was, after all, my—"

"I know," he broke in irritably. "You don't have to keep saying it."

"Of course," she said, and that meant Irene.

After another pause he asked her. "What will you do now?"

"I can't make any decisions yet," she said. "I have to have this baby first." She shook her head. "You see, even now I'm living for someone else. All my life, there was always someone. Before I came here – and then Frances, and then Ewan. And now, the baby."

The baby. Oh God, the baby. He wanted desperately to ask her then, but somehow he couldn't. He was afraid of the answer. Whichever way it was, it would hurt, and he couldn't decide for himself even in the abstract which way would hurt most.

She gazed at him calmly. It was impossible she shouldn't have known his thoughts, but she only said, "Ewan said, before he died, that if it was a girl, I ought to call it Livilla. Unusually witty, for Ewan."

She did not touch herself, or look down, or smile proudly, as other pregnant women seemed to. She seemed to bear the baby as a separate burden from her, as she had borne the last months of Ewan's life.

"But what will you do?" he asked again. He hoped, obscurely, that she would appeal to him, but he should have known better.

"Have the baby. And then – I think perhaps I'll try living for myself. It would have the attraction of novelty, if nothing else. I've always sublimated my ambitions until now – perhaps I'll try letting them have free rein."

"Writing?"

She smiled wryly. "Let's not fool ourselves. I haven't the talent. That was just an agreeable hobby. I think it's time I put it aside and faced the real world."

She would not touch the subject that really mattered. He had to force the issue. He said desperately, "But what about us? Now that you're free—"

"But you see, you're *not* free." She said it without rancour, as a matter of fact.

"I could be," he said. At that moment Irene and the boys seemed only an inanimate burden that he could cut free and drop on the path behind him.

"No, Hamil – no, you couldn't. I know you think it would be

easy, but you're attached to them, more than you think. It wouldn't work. And it would be wrong."

"Morally?"

"Yes, I think so. Not for some men, I know, but for you it would be. The guilt would haunt you and make you miserable, and then you'd hate me for it."

"I'd never hate you."

"You'd blame me. You don't need me enough, or Irene little enough, for it to be worth it to you."

"How do you know what I need?" he said angrily. "Don't decide my life for me. I need *you*. Don't you understand?" She watched him steadily. "I'm lonely," he cried.

"I know," she said quietly. "I am too – lonely for you. I love you more than I can bear, but we can't be together."

Those were the last, the only private words he spoke with her. The following day he had been obliged to go back to London, to work, to his wife and children, leaving her in Edinburgh. Word came to him after that as news of home to an exile who, though hostilities are long over, knows he will never now go home. He had settled in another country, home was far away, and the companions of his exile were now more real to him than the dearer people in the shadowy land. Never touching the loneliness, always slightly foreign to him, yet he learned the language and sometimes forgot that it was not his own native tongue.

He worked hard and conscientiously on Ewan's symphonic poem, to get it into a fit state to be published. Copies were sent to leading critics and musicologists, to Auerbach and to the musical directors of the main orchestras interested in new work. Hamil himself could achieve no firm opinion of his own about the quality of the piece, of where it might stand in the universal repertoire; and the experts who saw it were divided sharply over it. Auerbach, as perhaps was understandable, thought it a work of outstanding genius; at the other end of the spectrum Morgenstern of the New York Phil found it "confused; uneven; overlong; in parts brilliant; often unplayable".

Whatever the differences of critical opinion, the "unplayableness" seemed a sticking point with everyone Hamil approached. After a while, given the pressure of his own career, he handed it to an agent to try to get it performed, recorded or both, but nothing came of his endeavours either. In time Hamil felt able to let it go. Ewan's first three symphonies were still occasionally played: perhaps one day there would be a Strathearn revival and the symphonic poem would be resurrected from the archives and given air. At least, he felt he had done his best; he should be free of it now.

Livia's baby was christened Gillian, after Mrs Strathearn, but was known as Livilla – perpetuating, rather artificially, Hamil always thought, Ewan's Last Joke. Soon afterwards, Livia herself went on her travels. The baby stayed with her grandmother, who adored her and probably spoiled her, and who took on a new lease of life from her grandchild – if not the first, indisputably the dearest.

Frances, jealous of the baby's importance and hurt that it was not she that was asked to look after Livilla, married, out of spite, the steady, kindly, nondescript man who had been courting her all these years and whom Livia had once referred to, unflatteringly, as "something called Bill". This of course put Frances into an ideal position to fight for possession of Livilla, and since she was half her mother's age and had twice her energy, it looked as though there was going to be an interesting battle one of these days.

How Mr Strathearn felt about the child, Hamil never knew, nor could he speculate. Hamil always vaguely supposed that his father, out of his sympathy with Olivia, must have some thoughts about the origins of the child. Nevertheless, as with all his own children, he behaved towards his grandchildren with polite indifference, and Livilla, though thrust more insistently upon his attention than the others, was not excepted.

And now he had died, had suffered the fate that Hamil had dreaded for himself, had feared might have been exclusively set aside for him as his father's heir. To die lonely seemed to Hamil the worst possible thing; to die unfulfilled, shut out from the secret garden; perhaps, in his father's case, without ever having discovered it, only dreaming that it might exist, and then only for others.

Enough, he decided at this point in his thoughts, was enough: he had not arrived at the age of discretion only to deny himself his pleasures. He stood up.

"I'm going to the buffet," he said politely to Irene. "Do you want anything?" The children's heads went up. Strange how they associated food so exclusively with themselves.

"A cup of tea, perhaps," Irene said firmly, hoping to pass on the hint.

The children saved him from having to notice it by jumping in with, "Can we have some crisps, Dad?" and, "Can we come, Dad?"

Hamil considered. Of course, there was no reason why they shouldn't have crisps. Equally there was no reason why they should. His decision, either way, would be entirely arbitrary, but he felt children ought to have to contend with arbitrary disappointments. It was good for them – part of their training for later life.

He hesitated long enough for them to lose hope, and then said, "All right, you can have crisps. But you can't come with me."

"Please, Dad!"

"Why not, Dad?"

Irene, though no doubt wanting them to accompany him, reacted true to her code and said, "That's enough. If your father says no he means no."

Such, Hamil considered as he swayed along the train, are the lies with which we are indoctrinated through childhood. As if he himself ever meant exactly what he said!

* * *

It was Frances who opened the door to them.

"Well, well, well," she said vaguely, looking from Hamil to Irene. "And the children," she added without welcome.

She seemed at a loss for something to say, and Irene, her amazing social sense never failing her, took her hand and squeezed it and murmured, "Dear Frances. Don't try to say anything. We understand."

Thus prompted, Frances fell back from the door and let them in. She had taken to wearing glasses recently, yielding at last to the family myopia, and behind their thick shells of glass her eyes had lost their dreamy, milky look and were disconcertingly sharp. Hamil knew that he ought to say something along the same lines as Irene, but he could find nothing in Frances to which he could relate. She was so changed. She had never regained her figure after her pregnancy, and Frances fat was almost a contradiction in terms. And she had cut her hair, club-cut it like short fur. Hamil smiled weakly, and her sharp, blind eyes passed over him.

Douglass came into the hall. "Oh, there you are, Hamil. Thank heaven."

She at least had not changed, was still the same tall, severely beautiful, successful Douglass, as much a social animal as Irene – the two could have been from the same litter.

Hamil went forward to kiss her enamelled cheek. "Why thank heaven?"

"I don't think I could bear anything else to go wrong. Your train's late, of course, but one has come to expect that. Hello, Irene, you're looking well. Hello, boys. You'd better run and wash your hands and faces after your journey, and then you can go and play quietly in the nursery." Fergus and Francis, blitzed as usual by Aunt Douglass's efficiency, removed themselves without a murmur.

"Are your two there?" Hamil asked, watching them go, with a private smile at the thought that it might have been himself and Frances ordered off by their mother.

"Oh yes; and I'm hoping they'll stay there. Mother can be so difficult. She slops over them, and it makes Wolf cough."

Hamil had never been able to like either of Douglass's children. Angela was one of those stout, bossy, spiteful little girls who never seem to be really young. She was remarkably plain, and even Douglass had been known to express surprise at her daughter's lack of physical appeal. And Wolfgang was cave-chested and suffered from asthma, which ought to have won him everyone's sympathy, except that he was a whining, greedy child who used his weak chest as a cross between a bludgeon and a fishing-net.

"How's she taking it?" Irene asked, her voice weighted with sympathy.

"Mother? Oh, I don't think she really takes it in, you know. She didn't have much to do with him anyway, and it was so sudden – there was no illness, as with Ewan."

They followed Douglass into the drawing room, and at once Morton came forward to greet them with the expression of one being rescued. He shook their hands, desperately hospitable.

"Hello, hello! Good to see you. You must be drained after that journey. I don't know why, but they always seem to be digging up the London to Edinburgh track. Irene, you're looking more beautiful than ever. You must both want a drink – what will you have?"

It was strange to see Morton subduing his normal large voice and movements to suit the black occasion, but his warmth was genuine, and even Irene unbent a little. Hamil asked for whisky, and Irene for sherry, and while Morton arranged the drinks and chatted in a low voice to Irene, for whom he had always had a half-fatherly soft spot, Hamil went over to his mother, who was sitting in a chair by the fire.

He hesitated in front of her. It stunned him to see how much she had aged in the years since Ewan's funeral. She had shrunk and spread into a little, fat old lady – unmistakably old now, her hair quite white and her face starred with wrinkles like cracked ice. She clutched the arms of the chair with her white, freckled claws, and Hamil was moved to pity. She looked up at him, and he would have greeted her with a kiss, for the first time since childhood, but when he stooped to her she put her face away anxiously and looked about her.

"So you're here," she said. "And Irene? And the children? Ah, of course. I wish the others were here. I wish Livia would come back – there's so much to do. And I can't find my reading glasses. Well, Hamil, how are you? I don't need to ask – you always sailed through everything. Nothing ever troubled Hamil – the handsome one. *Did* you bring Irene with you?"

"Yes, she's here. And the boys."

"Well, at least *your* children have some manners." She threw a sharp glance at Douglass, who ignored it. "I expect they have Irene to thank for that. Where is she?"

"I'm here," Irene said, and came across to hunker in front of the old lady and engage her in conversation. Everyone loved Irene, Hamil thought, retreating gratefully – everyone except his father, that is. Father had neither liked nor disliked her. As with all people below a certain mental attainment, he had simply discounted her.

Hamil's eyes filled with tears again, and he turned away and walked to the window to twitch the curtain aside and look out. The same sliver of road, unchanged to the very texture of each brick. The same old movement of escape. The piano beside him was thick with dust. He didn't suppose Frances ever touched it now, and there was no one else to play it.

Douglass had gone out to Frances, and Morton came over to stand beside Hamil, eager for company. "I don't think the old lady properly takes it in," he said in a low voice. Hamil found it odd to hear a stranger refer to his mother as an old lady. He glanced over his shoulder, and, blurred by distance, she was just that. "It was so sudden."

Hamil didn't want to discuss his father's death, least of all with Morton. "Where's Fergus?"

Morton did not hear. "There are worse ways to go – a good, clean stroke, and finish. Not lingering on, a burden to yourself and your family—"

"Where's Fergus?" Hamil asked again, desperately. Morton gulped at his drink, moved by his own words.

"He's taken the little girl out. She was upset. Very sensitive to atmosphere. An intelligent child."

"Livilla?"

"Yes. He's taken her to the zoo, I believe. She was a great favourite with her grandpapa, of course."

"Was she? I'm surprised."

"Why surprised?"

"Father never had any time for children."

"Ah," said Morton wisely, "but she was different. Olivia's child."

Hamil stared at him, and then moved away abruptly to hide his face. "Where is Olivia?" he asked, his voice muffled by the lip of his glass.

"Well, that was kind of peculiar." Morton's voice came from behind him. "She'd been home for a while, and then she just suddenly took off without even saying where she was going. Rang up the next day, from New York. You know she works on and off for *Harper's* now, doing interviews?"

"No, I didn't," he said. He didn't know anything about her any more.

"Kind of freelance interviewer. Anyway, she phoned up to say she was doing an interview over there and would be back in a day or two. Left no number or address. And that same evening – well, it happened." A holy pause. "No one knows where she's staying, so no one can get in touch with her. We've left messages at the London and New York offices, and that's the best we can do, until she phones home. Kind of shook up the old lady, I guess, not being able to get hold of her. She relies on her a good deal, you know."

Hamil met Irene's eye, and she stood up, patting Mother's hand, and came over to him.

"You've heard about the mysterious disappearance, then?" she said. "It's just like her. She *would* be away just when she's needed. She always did things to suit herself."

A strange way to describe those years as Ewan's wife, Hamil thought, but he would not argue with Irene on that subject, in case he gave himself away. Morton joined them, and Hamil went back to the window to be alone. So Father had not even had that comfort at the last. To die alone and unloved seemed the cruellest of fates. "Good clean stroke", indeed! How did Morton know how long it took to die? To the dying man, helpless in a frozen body, each second might seem like a month, with help beyond reach. He began to cry, his shoulders shaking, and he held his breath rather than sob.

He heard behind him small exclamations, and then Irene's voice talking cheerfully to Mother. Talking to Mother, so that his crying should not be noticed. Irene protecting his dignity. She knew. She was a good wife. Through his tears he saw Fergus crossing the road towards the house, holding small Livilla by the hand.

Hamil had never had a daughter. Little girls all looked like that at that age: the short dainty coat, the slender, still-plastic legs ending in white socks and white sandals, the cropped fair hair, the grave, important way they conducted their small bodies and their affairs. Why did they have such power to move him? Since Livilla was born, all little girls were her. He must not let her be embarrassed by his crying. He escaped the room, and no one tried to follow him.

Later, when he had recovered his composure, he rejoined the family in the drawing room. The children had all been put to bed, and despite the occasion, much noise and merriment had ensued from the dormitory effect of the bedroom they still called the nursery.

Fergus greeted him with a handshake and asked after his work. "Irene's filled me in on all the news, so the question is a mere formality," he went on. "You're looking tired, old man. You're working too hard."

Now where had Fergus acquired that vestigial English accent? "Old man"? It must be part of his business front – strange how English accents were considered chic amongst the business class in Edinburgh.

"I have to work," he said. "I have a wife and family to support."

"Well, it won't do them any good if you go the way of poor Father," Fergus said. "Take my advice: take a rest. A break now and then makes all the difference. Look at me! I'm older than you, but I reckon I look younger."

"Yes, you do," Hamil discovered. "How do you manage that?"

Fergus tapped his nose. "Just take it easy, that's all. That's where Father went wrong – he wouldn't relax. These past few years he's driven himself unmercifully, and it took its toll."

"Only you can say, of course," Douglass interrupted calmly, "how hard he worked—"

"Just look at the state of the business; that will tell you," Fergus remarked.

Douglass went on without heeding his interpolation. "But as far as I can see, he behaved no differently at any other time of his life."

"You weren't here, living with him," Fergus said.

"Nor were you," Douglass retorted.

"Weren't you?" Irene asked him, surprised.

Fergus looked obscurely embarrassed. "That isn't entirely fair," he said. "I made one or two trips abroad, but that was all. And they were for the good of the business."

"Where abroad, Fergie?" Hamil asked.

"The States, mainly. There are lots of American firms setting up over here, and I wanted to be sure we got their business. So I went to make contacts and to study their methods. Nothing like speaking the same language."

The conversation drifted on to business methods and the American versus the British office systems, and Hamil's attention wandered until a question of Irene's drew it back.

"You had the handling of the will, I suppose?" she asked Fergus.

"Oh yes, of course. It was the one he made after Ewan died, with the alterations to make allowance for that. Nothing's been changed since then. Basically the business goes to me, and the house goes to Mother for her lifetime and to Frances afterwards. And everything else to Livia."

"Livia?" Hamil and Irene exclaimed almost simultaneously. They glanced at each other and Irene raised an eyebrow, which Hamil interpreted as *Why aren't you getting anything*? "Why to Livia, particularly?" he asked, trying to sound nonchalant. Had his father gone so far in his preference as to make it public?

"He felt that she was the only one left unprovided for, with Ewan dying, and his child to bring up. Frances and Bill are all right, Douglass and Mort have money to burn—"

"Catch me," Douglass said laconically.

"And you have your career, Hamil. So that only left Olivia and the little girl. Of course, there are small bequests to all of us, personal mementoes. But the bulk goes to them. Livilla will be a rich lady one day."

"But Livia had what Ewan left her," Hamil began, and broke off, because it sounded as if he begrudged her the bequest.

"Well, that wasn't much," Douglass said.

"Don't forget his royalties," Frances said scornfully. "His work must have been played hundreds of times in the last four years. Well worth dying for, wouldn't you say?"

"Shut up, Fan, this isn't the time," Douglass reproved her.

Frances still blamed Livia for Ewan's death, but she was even more bitter that Ewan had left his music to Hamil rather than to her, who had nursed him almost single-handed – until his last illness, when he would have no one but Livia near him. She was fated, she felt, always to do the donkey-work, and be left out of the unveiling ceremony. And if it had been left to her, she was sure she would have got Ewan's last work played somehow. She couldn't believe Hamil had really *tried*, and she said so now, vociferously.

It was in the middle of this family bickering that a key was heard in the front door, and everyone stiffened, knowing there was only one person who had a key and was not present. Eight pairs of eyes turned towards the door, but only Mother named the spectre.

"It's Livia!" she cried, half rising from her chair.

Livia appeared in the doorway, redolent of travel. Her clothes were the smart, comfortable garments of an experienced air traveller. She wore a capacious shoulder-bag of bruised leather and carried a duty-free carrier bag of exotic origin. Her hair was ruffled, her eyes bright, her face slightly smudged and worn with the long journey.

She regarded them all without speaking. No one knew what to say, how to tell her, what to choose to reprove her for; whether to welcome, condole or chastise. Fergus stood up – in his capacity as head of the family, Hamil imagined – and Livia's bright, shadowed eyes moved to him. She lifted her hand from the wrist in a tired gesture of negation.

"Is it all over?" she asked. There was a silence as people readjusted, but Hamil knew that she meant the funeral.

Fergus seemed to know also. He said, "No, it's tomorrow."

"Is he here?"

"No. We thought it best not."

"Ah." She gave a little quivering sigh and closed her eyes – with relief? – then opened them again and looked at the family one by one, seeming faintly amused. The expressions on their faces were perhaps rather amusing in the abstract – surprise and disapproval in about equal proportions.

Her eyes reached Hamil in turn, and her lips quirked in a ghost of a smile.

"Hamil," she said. He felt Irene look at him quickly, and tried not to colour.

"You knew?" he asked. She nodded.

"He knew. Ripeness is all. He told me."

"And you went away and left him?" Frances flared. Bill touched her hand, but she snatched it away.

"It was his idea," Livia said indifferently. It had been a long time since she had cared for Frances.

Mrs Strathearn caught her attention, and Livia went over and kissed her cheek.

"I'm glad you're back, Livia. I can't manage when you're not here. And I've lost my glasses again."

"We'll find them," Livia said. She straightened and turned back to the room where everyone still hung on her words. She stretched and grimaced, and her eyes sought Hamil again and, though he was feeding hungrily on every second of her, he was aware that it was dangerous, with Irene busy mathematising. "Oh, I'm so tired. I've been travelling all day."

"Come on," Fergus said. "I'll run your bath for you and get you something to eat. No – nobody else move. We'll manage."

He crossed to the door, gathering up Livia in his path and dropping an arm round her shoulders, and they went out together, shutting the door and leaving the room in silence. Hamil became aware that Frances was watching him, but as she opened her mouth to speak, Douglass slapped her hard on the wrist and said, "Shut up, Fan, and I mean it."

The uncomfortable evening looked like creaking on in this way. Hamil stood up and held out his hand to Irene.

"I think we'll turn in."

Perhaps no more surprised than touched, Irene rose too and came to put her hand in his. He rarely touched her in public, and she was gratified at this unexpected gesture.

"You're wise. Tomorrow's going to be quite a day," Douglass said grimly.

Hamil and Irene said goodnight and went in silence to their room. He knew there was more to come, and sure enough, when he was taking his turn in the bathroom, there came the discreet scratching at the door. He opened it, and Douglass slipped quietly in.

She locked the door again and sat on the bath edge. "One or two things you want explained," she began. "I've sat on Frances. I don't think she'll be letting any cats out of bags, but you never can tell. I'll keep my eye on her."

"I'm sorry, I'm a bit mazy," he said. "What was she about to say?"

"Oh, something about you and Livia, I suspect. She hasn't often been in company with you *and* Irene, so the opportunity hasn't arisen. Livia's no sense," she added shortly, "but I suppose it isn't to be expected. She will look at you, but with any luck Fergus will provide enough smokescreen to fox Irene and the rest of the family."

"Fergus? Why Fergus?"

"Hamil, I think you're a bit daft – or is it drunk?" Douglass said kindly. Her outline was blurring and dividing, so that she seemed to have a halo of herself around her. Was he drunk? A little, perhaps; drunk with emotions too. "You mean to say you didn't know about Livia and Fergus?"

"Know what about Livia and Fergus?" he said, but she didn't answer. She didn't have to. Slowly the tiny pieces fell together into the pattern. He knew what; it all made sense. "Oh God," he groaned very softly. He felt the sweat break out, cold in his armpits. "I think I'm going to be sick."

His head swung and rang like a gong and he stumbled to the pan as his nausea rose. He vomited, coughed, and vomited.

Distantly he felt Douglass's capable hands on his head and shoulder; distantly he heard her voice saying, "Too much drink and excitement." It was a motherly sort of thing to say. She had always been like a mother to him.

When it was over, he sat on the edge of the bath while she washed his face with a cold flannel and mixed him up some of Morton's special American mouthwash to take away the sour taste. She talked to him comfortingly, and got rid of Irene with great tact when she came to find him.

"Too much emotional strain," he heard her say to his wife.

"Too much drink," he heard Irene retort, but he sat staring at his hands and feeling nothing but his despair.

Ten

September 1980

The orchestra's van driver stopped him as he was walking into the hall before the concert.

"'Ere, Mr Straffon, there was a young lady asking for you this morning."

There was no one in Hamil's experience who could imbue any two words with so much significance as the driver did with "young lady". His face trembled on the brink of a wink and grimace; the curl of his lip suggested that she was at any rate no lady, and her youth was equally in doubt.

Hamil assembled and dismissed the possible ripostes and asked instead, seriously, "Did she leave any message?"

"No. She just asked for you, and I said you'd gone and I didn't know where you was. I told her about the concert tonight, so I daresay she'll be back, unless—" He allowed the end of the sentence to suggest itself. Unless she found easier prey. Unless she had found Hamil in the meantime. Unless she was waiting for him elsewhere.

"Seen her before?" Hamil asked casually. He certainly wasn't expecting anyone, but there were limitless possibilities. His question was designed to eliminate the chance that it was Irene, deciding to take a break after all.

"I ain't," Alf said succinctly, and turned away, whistling, to indicate the interview was over.

Probably one of the camp-followers, Hamil thought as he

headed for the dressing rooms – unless the whole episode was a figment of Alf's imagination. He, Hamil, hadn't anyone in tow at the moment, not since Lorraine, his luscious prize pupil, had graduated and got herself into the Hallé. On the other hand, perhaps it was one of his former little pigeons coming home to roost. Or how about Cathy, the American student he had met when they had played the Hollywood Bowl earlier that year? She said she might be coming to Britain, and had promised to look him up. It was better when his extra-curricular girls were music students, just in case they turned up at a concert to which Irene had decided to come. Gave him a viable excuse.

And he would welcome a little company now. Only a four-day tour, and Irene had stayed at home, and he didn't know a soul in this part of the world. Ideal.

"Oh, Hamil, there was a woman here this morning just after you'd gone, asking for you," he was told as he entered the dressing room.

"So Alf said. No message, I suppose?"

"No, she just went away. Nice looker, though, you lucky man. Relative?"

"How could I possibly know?" Hamil said, taking off his coat. "I've no idea who it was."

"You weren't expecting anyone then?"

"Nope. I hope to God she comes back, or I shall know no peace."

And at that point his companion looked over his shoulder and said, "Here she is now. I'll make myself scarce."

Hamil looked up, and saw Livia standing in the doorway. "It's all right, Bill, it's only family," he said, but Bill grinned knowingly and departed.

Olivia smiled at Hamil and crossed quickly to lift her face for a chaste kiss on the cheek.

"How are you?" she said. "And what do you mean, *only family*?"

"Livia," Hamil said, returning the kiss warily. "What are you doing in this neck of the woods?"

"Your vocabulary," she winced. "Neck of the woods, indeed! And you don't sound at all pleased to see me."

"You've surprised the socks off me," he said frankly. "I haven't had time to feel pleased yet. They said someone was asking for me, but of all the people I thought it might be, I never thought of you."

"Well, don't stand there staring at me like that," she said, and added crossly, "Come, Hamil, you surely must have grown out of your guilty conscience by now."

"It isn't that," he said hastily. "I told you, I'm surprised. I've got to go on and play in half an hour: you don't make it easy for me. What *are* you doing in this n – in these parts, anyway?"

"Oh, just passing through, you know. I was doing a job in Cardiff, and I saw your billing, so I detoured to take you in. I just missed you this morning, or we could have spent the afternoon together."

Her voice was warm and caressing, and he looked over her shoulder awkwardly.

"Don't, Livia, not now. I have to warm up before I go on and I'll never – look, I'll meet you afterwards, all right? Wait for me outside, will you?"

"Outside? Like one of your teenage groupies?"

"Please, Livia – you know what it's like," he begged. It was not unknown for things to get back to wives, and while he could talk his way out of a "teenage groupie"—

She looked sad. "Yes, I know. All right, I'll meet you outside. But don't hang around and keep me waiting in the cold."

"You can't really think I'd do that," he said, touching her arm. She looked at his hand, and then up at his face, and smiled, and went quickly away, understanding him.

When he came out of the concert hall after the concert she was waiting for him, discreetly, across the road and out of the lamplight. She fell in beside him like a conspirator, without word or gesture.

They walked a little way in silence, and then he said, "Thanks."

"It's all right," she said. "You're a fool, but – all right."

"I've got the car parked up here. We'll go to a pub – somewhere quiet."

"A car, eh? Not like the old days."

"Oh Livia—"

"I've my car too, but it can stay here. It's parked safely."

"I'll bring you back to it," he promised, and then wished he hadn't, for it seemed too final at this early stage. "Good concert?" he asked to cover his awkwardness. She grinned.

"Weren't you there?"

"You know what I mean."

"You were superb," she said. "I love the trumpet part in the last bit of Brahms Two. Makes the hair rise on the back of my neck; most especially when it's you playing it."

"Flatterer."

"Not a bit. I speak the pure truth."

He didn't speak again until they were out of town and driving along the coast road. He had been painfully aware of her in the darkness beside him, the scent of her so close in the car, where that scent was unfamiliar. The car smelt of Irene and the children and the dog. The jolt was like going up one stair too many. He wanted to touch her, wanted to lay his hand on her knee as he drove, to reassure himself of his sexual relationship with her, but he dared not. Anyway, the car's steering was heavy; he ought not to drive with one hand off the wheel. That was an excuse he could use to himself.

"I used not to be such a coward," he said at last, apologetically, as if she would know what he had been thinking. In the dark her hand pressed his leg in sympathy, withdrew, and then rested there lightly – tentatively.

"Things change," she said. "It can't be helped. You are glad to see me?"

"Of course. And you?"

"That's why I'm here."

They hadn't always needed such reassurances, he thought. "There's a pub along here somewhere, on the left. Keep an eye out for it. It's got a private bar – we can be quiet there." On the other hand, he thought, maybe they'd be happier for a little background noise, so that they weren't made too aware of the grinding gears of their own unaccustomed conversation. "Or would you rather go somewhere more – festive?"

"Whatever you say," she said non-committally.

"Ah, here's the pub. I was here a few years back. I suppose it'll be OK."

He parked the car and they crossed the yard in silence and entered the quiet pub. There was hardly anyone there – presumably most of their trade was done at weekends – and they chose a corner of the saloon bar as being private enough.

"The usual?" he asked her with an effort.

"Please," she said. She smiled, as if it gratified her to have him remember her usual drink. She sat down at the table while he went up to the bar, and he watched her covertly, out of the corner of his eye, as he waited to be served. She sat quite still – no fussy settling of skirt or handbag, no patting of the hair – but she turned her head this way and that, taking in the scene, committing to memory the few faces around the bar.

"Well, here we are then. Cheers." He seated himself, after a moment's thought, beside her, and she swivelled round a little to face him.

"Cheers," she said, and drank. Her eyes were all over him, hungry and smiling.

"You haven't changed a bit," he said somewhat lamely.

"You have," she replied.

"Not for the better, by the sound of your voice," he joked, passing a hand over his face. "The old wrinkles, eh? The grey hairs—"

"You never used to be so—" She paused to find the word.

"What?"

"Conventional."

"Conventional?"

"You're not at ease with me. You're behaving like everyone else. You, at least, were always different. What's happened?"

The years peeled away as he looked into her face. She hadn't changed – he had meant that – and in her he found a memory of himself, an echo of home.

"Exile," he said at last. "When was the last time, Livia? Father's funeral?"

"We were together then, even with Irene between us," she said.

"But I had to go away," he said. "I sat on the train and it went through the Calton Tunnel, and it was like the end of everything. All I could think of was the life I was going to, and how I was leaving behind everything I valued. You did that to me."

She shook her head, but didn't answer. She would not repeat the old arguments.

"I always thought," he went on, "that it was appropriate that Father should have left me out of his will – as if he recognised a sort of family pale that I was beyond." What good could Hamil carry away with him that would not shrivel and desiccate in the parched air of the south? "It was a case of two different worlds."

"He was the one thing that kept the family together," she said. "I don't think anyone realised it at the time, he always seemed so quiet and separate; but afterwards, without him, we all fell apart from each other like unbaled hay. Without him there was no home."

"But only you and I came away," he said, touching her hand again. Hers caught his and curled round his fingers, and they held hands under the table like young lovers. "Me to my exile, and you to – whatever you went to."

"But I was right, wasn't I?"

"Right about what?" He knew what, but didn't want to know.

"About Irene and the children. Yes, I was, you must admit it.

Look how you were with me for the first few minutes. They were more real to you than I was, just then."

"That's hardly fair. How would you have felt—"

"Not like that," she said. "But then, my life is very different anyway. Nothing is very real to me now, I think." She paused, reflectively. "How's your work?" she asked, tacking.

"Well—"

"You're still with the same orchestra," she remarked.

He looked defensively sideways at her.

"It's the best symphony orchestra in the world. And we are doing some very interesting things. We get the best artists, we tour, we've more recording contracts than anyone else. And there's not much solo work for trumpet, you know that." She said nothing, merely raised an eyebrow, waiting for him to be honest with himself. But, damn it—! "I mean it," he said. She looked away from him and took a sip of her whisky. "It isn't so easy, you know, not when you've a wife and kids and so on. You can't afford to—"

"That's what's so sad," she said. "Not being able to afford to. For my money, orchestral trumpet's the best there is. If you were content with things as they are, it wouldn't matter."

"Well, what the hell do you expect me to do?" he exploded.

She merely shrugged. "I said nothing."

"What are you doing these days?" he asked after a moment, with an effort to be polite.

"The same," she said with a grimace. "Interviews. Articles. Consumer write-ups. The occasional short story – that's the height of my creativity." She made a downwards *moue*. "A boy-meets-girl shortie – three thousand words of escapist pap."

"Poor Livia; does it hurt?" he teased her.

"You don't know how much," she said lightly. "Still, it pays the rent. And it's better than being a personnel officer."

"What name do you write under?"

"You mean you don't know?" she mocked him. "In some parts of the world, Olivia Strathearn is a household name."

"What parts?" he challenged.

"Oh, Ruislip Gardens, perhaps. Ashton-under-Lyne. Frances reads them, you know, my soupy stories. Only in secret. I've seen her sneaking the mag into the lavvie sometimes."

"Why the lavvie?"

"She's ashamed of reading anything so unintellectual – legacy of your mother's prejudices. She puts on a brave show in public. 'Goodness, no!' she says." Her voice was an exact parody of Frances's Morningside drawl. "'I can't be bothered with *that* sort of thing.' Poor Fanny."

"I'm surprised you use Strathearn instead of Porsen," Hamil said.

"Are you? But I'm so much a part of your family it's hardly feasible to distinguish any more."

"What about your old ambitions, to sail round the world and write a great novel? You haven't given that up, have you?"

"What a romantic you are! I'm sorry to let you down, but one says that sort of thing in the heady days of youth. I'm a writer of articles about the relative merits of different washing machines, that's all. It's a rotten job, but someone has to do it." She smiled as she said it, but he felt saddened.

"You used to be so confident," he said.

"So did you. I told you it'd get you in the end."

"I can't remember what *it* that was," he said. "But it got me all right. What got you?"

She sighed. "I just had to face up to it that I had no talent of any sort. I'm very ordinary. But it's not so bad, you know. After what I watched Ewan go through, I feel positively grateful not to be brilliant." She mused. "And yet – he did give me a sort of significance as a person. Inspiring him, driving him on to complete his masterpiece – in universal terms I suppose you could see it as the apogee of my life."

"Is that how you see it?" He was appalled.

"I don't know. I'll have to see what the rest of my life holds." She reflected. "Poor Ewan. What a time he had. Pushed by your mother from birth practically, and then hounded by me. I feel so terribly guilty sometimes. His death was suicide really, you know."

"Suicide?" Hamil asked, startled. What had he not been told?

"He killed himself with drink, drugs and all the rest of it. I think he couldn't live with the fear that he wasn't going to make it. That perhaps he wasn't the genius everyone had always expected him to be."

Hamil could sympathise with that. Other people's expectations, he thought, both defined and confined you – unless you were a very brave sort of person, brave enough to face them down. "His symphonic poem has never been performed, you know," he said.

"I know. Frances hates you for that. She thinks you didn't try. Oh, yes, I know you did. But perhaps it's better that it hasn't been performed. If it had been, and flopped, think how devastating. No, at least this way she and your mother can cling on to the myth of his greatness."

"Myth? Don't you think he *was* great, then?"

"I'm the wrong person to ask. I don't know enough about music – and I have a vested interest in believing he was. Living with him was such hell, and I felt so ashamed of myself – for having done it, you see. So he had to be a genius to justify it for me."

"If it helps," Hamil said, "I think he was."

She looked away for a moment, but squeezed his hand under the table gratefully. "Yes. I think it does help. Thanks."

In the gentle silence that followed, all the old regrets surged up. "You should have come to me when Ewan died," he said suddenly. "We could have done it then. We could have made the break."

She shook her head. "You can't rewrite the past like a script. It wouldn't have worked, then. You were still too undecided. And you resented my having married Ewan in the first place."

"I still do. I resent every scrap of love you've given my family. Except my father. You didn't love him enough."

Olivia looked startled. "What on earth do you mean?"

"You left him when, by your own admission, you knew he was going to die."

She didn't answer straight away. She was thinking of the old man, unexpectedly, for the first time in years, and it saddened her.

"Hamil, he sent me away," she said. "Believe me, it was his idea."

"You shouldn't have gone, then," Hamil said. "He was only testing you. You let him die alone." In his anger with her was all his own horror of that terrible end.

"He wanted it that way. My God, do you think I would have left him otherwise? After all—" She broke off abruptly.

Their eyes met, and quite suddenly Hamil understood something that had been on his mind since the first year of their acquaintance. It had been a little niggling puzzle he had carried with him since that day long ago that he had met her in his father's office, and utterly failed to understand what was going on.

He stared at her, and the words burst from him. "You were his lover, weren't you?"

She was silent, as if calculating his reaction; then, "Yes. Right at the beginning. He was the first – that's how I met Frances. I never would have, otherwise – we weren't in the same school, after all. But he wanted me to get friendly with her, take her out of herself, broaden her social horizons. He was worried because she had so few friends."

Hamil shook his head as a dog shakes water out of its ears. "So that was it. Then she brought you to the house. And then—"

"Oh God. Please don't, Hamil. It seems my whole life has been bound up with one member of your family or another."

"Including Fergus?"

"What?" She seemed startled.

"You and Fergus. That hurts, you know. Don't you discriminate *at all*?"

"I've never been to bed with Fergus. What are you talking about?"

"At Father's funeral. Douglass said – and I saw you together. You certainly looked intimate. He put his arm round your shoulders."

She shook her head in amused wonder. "What does Douglass know? And of course Fergus and I are intimate: I've known him a very long time. He's my brother-in-law, for goodness' sake! I love him very dearly as a brother, but—" She shook her head again. "I firmly believe he's still a virgin, you know. He's one of nature's celibates, like a dear old don, pottering about an Oxford college. Except that he's also a natural family man, and very fond of children. An odd contradiction, but all the more endearing for that."

Hamil was silent, feeling a fool, but also feeling hugely relieved. In his relief about Fergus, he had forgotten about his father.

"How long have you been harbouring that particular resentment?" she enquired after a moment.

"I'm sorry I said you didn't discriminate," he said with a faint, rueful smile.

"So I should hope." She leaned towards him a little, and said seriously, "It was you I loved. Always."

"Really?" he asked, taking up her hand which was resting on the table.

"How can you doubt it? How can I convince you?"

"I could try to think of something." He drew her hand down and laid it over his fly.

"Hamil, for God's sake, you can't do that in a pub!" she protested, laughing. "You'll get us arrested. No, no, stop. Go and get another drink."

"It's your round. Aren't you a liberated lady?"

"All right, if you insist."

"No, I don't want another drink anyway. I want to go somewhere private, with you."

She smiled into his eyes, a remote and passionate smile, like a remembered mistress.

"Where had you in mind?"

They went back to his hotel. Most of the orchestra were staying there, but Hamil's fear of being seen had dwindled to the point where he could even walk in with her instead of going ahead and telling her to follow. Luck was with him, and they met no one on the stairs or in the corridor.

"Hotel smell," she said as he unlocked the door to his room. "Biscuits and Windsor soup and dust and Airwick. Every hotel I have ever known smelled like that. Memoirs of a lost girlhood. I have measured out my life in coffee spoons." He opened the door and she followed him into the dark. "I often wondered as a girl what a coffee spoon was."

"I've often wondered if you had a girlhood," he said. He turned on the light and she leapt into being by the door, screwing up her eyes against the glare, for a moment disarmingly human and unstudied.

"How long is it?" she asked, walking towards him.

"How long is what?" he asked her, surprised. "Turn the lock," he said nervously. She reached behind her and did so without looking.

"How long since we made love?"

"I don't know. A long time – too long. Do you think we'll remember how?"

For answer she slid her hands inside his jacket. He closed his arms round her and kissed her, trying to remember what it was like. Her mouth seemed strange to him, hard where Irene's was soft, an alien taste, unremembered, wicked. It was fornication, of course, that corked-wine taste of the forbidden act, a delight in sin perpetually renewable. He closed his eyes and thought of Polly, Ann, Isobel, Lorraine, Cathy, of his multiple transgressions, but it was only the one act, the same, infinitely protracted. *Hell is anything forever? Don't you believe it, my son! The virtuous in heaven, so they say, enjoy thousand-year orgasms on heated airbeds.*

His licensed hands roved, and he edged round the bed, reached for the light and turned it off. He pressed her down on to the candlewick and stretched himself beside her. In the dark there was no sound but their breathing and the intermittent protest of the bedsprings and the rustle of various garments parting and lifting. The alien mouth grew familiar, his hand met forgotten skin, goose-fleshed in the intemperate air of an English hotel bedroom in September. The alien body grew a hand which inched towards his sub-tropical zones, and he eased over on to his side and cursed softly as the springs groaned again.

I have measured out my life on hotel beds, he thought. She smelled good – what was it? He stuck his head into her neck and snuffled.

"What's that scent you use? Le Bois?"

It was a mistake to speak. Her body was a body in the dark. All cats are grey. But her voice was her own.

"Still Le Bois. You have a good memory."

She was Livia, Olivia, from the past, his brother's wife, real and formidable in the dark; not anonymous and obliging, to be taken pleasure of without words, the girl he might have picked up for the purpose that Alf thought she was. She was herself, she was – oh God, it all hurt too much! All that she was rose up in the darkness like a wave to overwhelm him. Olivia – here. Olivia and Ewan. Ewan – dying. Father – dying.

"What's wrong? What is it?" she whispered. He clutched at her shoulders with rigid hands, but he could find no possible words to answer her with, as the great breaker of pain and despair crashed over him.

"What's the matter?"

"Olivia."

"Yes! Darling, darling, I'm here. What is it?"

His hands bit into her shoulders, but he could not make it real. His body, stretched out against hers, was clumsy and vulnerable.

In this dark anything might come and take him, ravening mouths snatch at him. God was watching, God knew what was in his heart. As a child he had been in terror of a God that knew his thoughts and condemned him for them, even though he could not help them, had no control over them. It was like being hastened towards a gallows for a crime he hadn't committed, hurried along by big rough hands. He could not reach her, though he felt her hands stroking his body, trying to comfort him, and realised he was crying.

"Darling, Hamil, what is it? It's all right, darling."

"Livia, I can't," he said, out loud, at last.

"I know," she said. "It doesn't matter." She knew. Had felt him limp and helpless beside her. *Not that – that wasn't what I meant.* "It's all right," she said.

It wasn't all right, would never be, perhaps had never been. Not for Ewan, dying in the dark. *We never kept our promises.* And Father, not for him. *Alone in the end, because we'd all gone away.* Dying alone, forsaken, the end of a bitter, barren life. Douglass and her dull husband, unloved, and her unlovely children. Frances bitter, hating everyone. Livia alone. Hamil alone.

"It's not all right. It's what we always say – lies to the children. We should teach them what it will really be like."

"We don't know. Maybe it will be all right for them," she said. "We don't know."

"It can't be. How can it?"

"Darling," she said helplessly. "I can't bear to see you cry."

"It was your fault," he said. She shook her head in denial. He felt the movement. "You went away. You married Ewan."

"It wasn't that," she said. "That wasn't what changed things."

He rolled away from her, on to his back. His resentment against her was hard inside him, the only force left in him, the only direction. He wanted to punish her. What might he have been if she had not made those bad decisions? It was her fault. He put his arm over his face to press the ridiculous tears back. Even this, this evening, was her fault. He couldn't even—

"It comes to something," he said, muffled by his arm, trying to sound normal, "when I can't even screw. The one thing I'm famous for."

"Don't," she said out of the darkness. "Don't try to distance yourself from me." A polite, English voice, cool and warm together. What did she think? What did she really feel?

"It's not your fault," he said at last.

"It isn't," she said, "but I wonder if *you* realise that."

"Is it too late?"

"It's never too late. You only have to want to."

"I always wanted to. It's just that there were always other things that had to be done."

"I know."

Other things. Irene and the boys. Yes, they were extremely other. And what about—?

"Livia," he said, "what about the baby?" The pillow rustled as she turned her head towards him. "What about Livilla?"

"Not such a baby any more," she said – a cautious answer.

The thing he wanted to ask rose only as far as his throat, and choked him. He was so afraid of the answer. If it were the wrong answer, how could he live with it?

Instead, at last, he said, "I saw her only once, a little girl in white socks and sandals." He saw her a hundred times a year: every little girl he passed made him turn his head, hungrily. "But I forget she's growing all the time. She had fair hair like you. Does she still look like you?"

"Her hair's darker now, and her eyes are blue. No, I think she has a Strathearn face."

"Any particular Strathearn?" He wished at once he hadn't asked it.

But she said, judiciously, "She looks like your father, mostly. Like you."

He didn't know what she meant by that, and he was too afraid to ask. He heard his own breath drawn in shakily. "Does she – is she clever?"

"I think so. But she hasn't any particular talent. She's like me in that respect. As far as one can tell, of course – she's only ten, after all. But Strathearn talent shows itself early, doesn't it?"

He turned to her then. "You have a talent," he said. "People love you – that's a talent."

"Do they? It seems to me rather that people need me."

"Isn't that the same thing?"

He heard the smile in her voice as she said, "That rather depends which side of the need you are."

He reached for her, drew her into his arms, and she came willingly, folding into the angles of his body like water flowing, as if they had slept together every night of their lives.

"Stay with me tonight," he said.

"Now where did you think I was going to sleep?" she enquired, amused. He pressed his lips to her hair and held her close; close and dear to him – oh, so very dear.

They fell asleep, and woke at first light, and made love. From the warmth of sleep they slipped easily into it, and there was no strain, no effort, nothing to prove or fear, merely the warmth of two curled animals with the same name and the same smell. He dozed again with her in his arms, her head on his shoulder, utterly content.

The light strengthened outside and the day gathered pace, and it was necessary to move. He dreaded the necessity.

"We have to get up," he said.

"No," she murmured from her comfortable position.

"I have to go to work."

She rolled over on to her back, her eyes on his face, and he followed her over, leaning above her on one elbow.

"Good morning," he said, and kissed her. It was meant to be a light, departing sort of kiss, but it was hard to stop once he had begun. Her hand slid down his flank and he moaned a little through their joined mouths. "I really do have to go."

"Soon. Not yet."

No, not yet. He slid over on top of her and she clasped him in her arms. There was no difficulty now. The spectres had all departed; he was lying in the sunshine with his mistress in the sweet hour of waking together. He loved her, it was good, his sweat was good. Even when he got up at last, leaving her curled and damp in his rumpled bed, the mood was not broken. It was not too late – it was never too late. Not for them. There was always this between them, infinitely renewable.

Breakfast was over by the time they went down, and almost everyone was gone. Almost – they were seen. "I don't care," he said. It was almost true. He wished he had the right to ask her where she was going. It was sunny and he was hungry. "I wish I didn't have to go to work," he said wistfully.

"Do you? Have to, I mean?"

"Yes."

"There's your answer, then."

"But we still have the drive up to the car park, where you left your car."

"We still have that," she agreed gravely.

There were more people to see them as he parked the car by the hall and let her out. He straightened proudly and walked with his shoulder touching hers. He went with her to her car, watched her get in, closed the door for her. She did not say where she was going, and he did not ask. It seemed strange to see her in a driving seat, putting the key in the ignition, checking the mirror, all familiar movements, but not associated with her. He bent to kiss her goodbye through the window, a soft kiss, a familiar mouth.

"Hamil," she said suddenly, looking up at him, frowning against the sun behind him, "there's only you. There was only ever you – no one else."

"Yes," he said. "I know."

He waved goodbye as she drove away, and she waved back, a hand flapping out of the open window. He was reminded of his sons.

Eleven

April 1984

The small irritations of the day built up into the hot anger of an unburst boil, and he seethed, frustrated as a tethered dog, all the long tube journey. He felt as if he had been flayed, that any touch would be agony, and yet he had to stand pressed nose to back with a solid mass of sour-smelling humanity for twenty minutes. At each station the doors eased open and, as a torturer pauses to allow the jangling nerves to slip back on to the raw side of numbness, so for a moment the crowd would slacken and allow him to draw a dry breath, to turn his face away from the armpit of the tall man in the business suit. Just for a moment – and then the newcomers would press inwards with the enthusiasm of freshmen on their first pub-crawl.

At Liverpool Street he allowed the pressure to carry him like a current out and up into the mainline station, and drop him. He looked at his watch. Twenty minutes before his train. A drink? He glanced towards the station bar. It was bare and dirty, and peopled by unshaven men in filthy clothes who surely lived there, surely could not be travellers, for they had no look of impermanence, no mezzanine air of being between stages of a journey.

He hesitated, wanting a drink, emphatically *not* wanting that place; and as his hesitation extended itself he recognised, fleetingly, the chronic inability to decide of the young Frances. But he had no Olivia here to carry him through. He made a random movement and let his feet take him into the bar. Once through the door old habit took over.

"Scotch," he said. Say "please" in a British Rail buffet and you'd be laying yourself open to short measure and overcharging. Only the tenderfoot said please.

The glass hit the bar top and skidded a little towards him, slopping the yellow liquid greasily up the side of the glass. The light threw into sharp relief the frieze of finger-marks round the rim of the glass, and changed the natural amber of the whisky to the colour of urine. Hamil's fingers moved reluctantly. Surely he could not be going to put that in his mouth? There was a hot pain behind his eyeballs that hardened to bakelite when he closed his eyes and took hold of the glass. The smell of the whisky came to him, authentic and sharp across the stale reek of the place, and he brought the glass up blindly to his mouth and swallowed.

Pepper to the roof of the mouth. Hard and tasteless to the throat, burning as it reached the top of the chest, and then the foreign, scented, wheaten taste flooding back up into the mouth. Two tears burst painfully past his tear ducts and he blinked them back, opening his eyes and coughing a little. He looked down into the glass tentatively and oh, God was good to him, there was still a whole mouthful left.

Like cells grouping, his discordant parts began to reassemble, obedient to the familiar stimulus. The squalor of the bar faded, sight, sound and smell, with the change of his focus from outside in to inside out. He placed his elbows carefully, carefully, on the edge of the bar, and eased his weight on to them, and sought across the gulf his image in the dim mirror behind the optics. They found each other out, Hamil and reflection. *Ah, sweet Jesus, is that what we look like?* That round, whitish face, like the uneven cliff of unsalted butter on the marble slab of the grocer in Sciennes; slightly gleaming, with the moist look of wax, and marked into rough features by the grocer's wooden palette.

No one – *no one* – sells butter like that any more. The memory was from so long ago that it stood up distinct and incredible like an historical fact, isolated from association so that he could not tell if he had been four or fourteen the last time he had watched the grocer slap up a half-pound of unsalted and wrap it in his own printed paper. How remote that world was; how far from any present significance his childhood and his family. They could not exist in this modern world – they could not breathe its thin air. Quirkily individual, they sported against the rich exotic fabric of immutable Edinburgh.

There they were still, in his mind, unchangeable and spicily, darkly foreign: his own kin, but the more exciting for the shared blood. And he was here, in exile: a pale face, features soft with erosion; eyes pink with strain around the faded blue; fine hair not so dark now, failing and threaded with silver.

The soft blurred features looked back at him sadly. *Well might you be sad!* He addressed an ironic salute of the glass towards that diminished figure. Where was the vivid, familiar individual he could remember smirking back at him from bathroom mirrors? He never saw himself in bathroom mirrors now. He looked in the mornings, but saw only the state of the shallow rash along his jaw-bone – his skin had become so sensitive that to shave was an agony, yet the sight of himself unshaven hurt a vanity deeper than the skin.

They had all had lovely skin as children. Lovely, pale skin and dark hair – his father's gift – and blue eyes from his mother. Like the seven fairies, they had bestowed what they had at each christening. But whom had they offended? Someone had not been invited, some gatecrasher had taken out a grim endowment for the children, to mature at puberty. And the youngest, Ewan, like the youngest in fairy-tales, had been especially marked out. He, Hamil, had got off lightly, he supposed, if you could call survival getting off lightly.

I have lived too long, he thought. *I ought to have had the pride not to endure*. And yet, half smothered in the fat of his soul was something that still lifted its head in curiosity. Like a fly embedded in a pat of lard. The whitish face opposite him smiled, and he saw the shadow of that sloping, enmeshing smile that had sought out the carnal thoughts of young lady music-lovers on four continents. How they had loved to sublimate their devotion to the muse! How he had led them on, coaxing them into arpeggios up and down his relaxed and smiling body. How they loved music, they cried, how they lo-o-o-ved Brahms, adored Tchaikovsky; music was all, they cried, while he plundered their aesthetic libidos in anonymous hotel beds.

The unmusical *tong* of the station announcement brought his eyes back into focus through the golden haze he had spun for himself. Had it been like that? He could hardly remember across the years. They didn't rush to meet him at the stage door now. He would have to do a lot more talking now, if the occasion ever arose. But it didn't. Nothing arose any more. After work he went home, just like everyone who wasn't a musician.

Musician, my God! That was a joke. Half blind, wholly defeated, he sat at the back of the orchestra, more at one with his chair than with his soul, and hacked away at music he no longer heard, fighting to keep his seat against the hot young Turks coming out of the colleges, more of them every year. Where had all the passion gone? Was each man endowed with just so much, that when it had been spent, there was no more? Young Turks beware!

He struggled. It couldn't be true. He wasn't old yet, not inside. Even outside he was only *just* not young – not even really middle-aged yet. And then he smiled sardonically. *Christ, if you see so many spectres in a single whisky, you'll be out of your mind before the evening's out.*

He glanced again at his watch. Time to go get a place, before the last-minute rush of the weekenders join the painful swelling of the daily commuters. He picked up his instrument case – a beautiful, casual gesture with all the beauty of rightness, like a woman picking up a child – and walked out.

One whisky had been enough to restore his introspection. As he crossed the station his eyes sought his own image in every reflective surface with all the comfort of an accustomed pleasure. He watched himself with ironic love, sideways, in the windows of the train. It was going to be crowded. Automatically he counted, calculated, noted the lack of empty seats. He had delayed a little too much. There were no seats. He would have to stand.

The man immediately in front of him stopped abruptly to open a door and get in, forcing Hamil to a standstill. He was beside the buffet. Fate! Well, if he was going to have to stand, he might as well stand in the buffet queue as anywhere else. The end of the queue had buried itself in the corridor. He walked on to the next doorway, got in, and slid into place at the end of it.

It did at least give one a sense of purpose. People thrust slowly past in either direction with the pointless milling of cattle in a pen. The same faces came past each way, having walked in hope to one end and retraced their steps in resignation. If one of them would have the sense to pass on the message that there were no seats they could all stand still where they were. But perhaps they needed a sense of purpose too. Who was he to deny them? Anchored to his queue, he lounged with the superiority of one who has latched on to the inevitable early enough to secure an advantage.

Now the train was moving. It had picked up from nothing with no sense of transition. He remembered the lovely lost days of steam, when trains started with a jerk that sent you flying into the arms of the lady opposite and slung a spoonful of your martini over the edge of your glass. He missed the resonant, grinding grunt, grunt, grunt-grunt, picking up speed weightily, so that you really felt you were embarking on an adventure, going somewhere important that would have an irrevocable effect on your own life and perhaps the course of history.

But the modern trains had been streamlined into blandness. That was in tune with the age, in which nothing must stand out or be different, everything must be homogenised, sterilised, comfortably insipid. Modern life must be safe, even at the cost of terminal boredom.

Nothing violates my nature but boredom.

He heard Olivia's voice saying those words as clearly as in a silence. That was twice in the space of ten minutes he had thought about her. Three times makes a truth. *Hear a new word, you'll hear it again within the day.* He ached suddenly with loneliness. The queue jerked forward, and fatigue shut down over his mind and eyes, automatic defence against such aches. He had heard once, somewhere, that women – wives, that is – work out their shopping lists and their chores for the next day while their husbands are making love to them. As he lurched forward with each convulsion of the queue he ran over the next day's scores, planned his timetable, worked in such home chores as were inevitable, and reluctantly crossed out things he was definitely not going to have time for.

Automatically he pressed himself backwards to allow those who had been served to pass him, drawing in his shoulders and trying to make his case smaller. But now the person was not passing him, was standing, obstructively, in front of him. Holding up a can of beer and a plastic cup as if offering them to him. He tried to shrink another inch; and then his absent eyes made contact, and a voice tuned in, slowly.

"Take it, will you? I need a spare hand. There's more room out in the corridor."

He kept looking and making no sense of it. *Could* a person dream as realistically as this? Could he have gone mad and feel as sane as he did?

"Olivia?" he said at last, and it came out as a question, almost querulously. She looked at him patiently, still holding out the can and cup, looking as unsurprised as if she had been travelling with him all along. She had bought him a beer – she must have known he was there. But how? His mind revved, out of gear. "How did you get here?"

She glanced around her. "I practised," she said. Obedient at last to her urging he took the offered drink, glancing down at it, puzzled, and up at her again.

"But how did you know I'd be here?"

"I didn't. Why should you think I did? Oh – the beer." Her face was luminous, with humour, perhaps, or pleasure. "That's simple – I asked the man for two, to save having to queue again, and he assumed I wanted two cups as well, so I didn't bother to argue. Then, coming back, I saw you. I've a couple of miniatures in my pocket as well. Scotch. Come, we're blocking the way."

She urged him, as she spoke, out of the buffet car and into the comparative space of the corridor. He turned at last, by the carriage door, and looked at her. It was – years, he didn't know how many – since they had last met. He could not tell if she had changed, looked better or older, or even if she had her hair done the same way. Her face was simply a thing he could recognise: it was as familiar as her voice, but it had its own continuity. As he could never recall her when she was not there, so, present, she was the only reality.

She tucked herself into the corner opposite him, and drew a long, shaky breath.

"Oh, but it's good to see you again," she said. Her lambent eyes were all over his face, in that way he remembered that shook his bones; from the very beginning, coming too close under his skin.

"How are you these days?" he asked, inadequately. "Still writing?"

She made a face, at the question and the form of it. "Still writing my rubbish. Articles mostly. A few short stories. You have to have "feisty" heroines these days, but they're still all looking for true love." Her face lit up with a sudden humour. "The blessed innocent of an editor changed the title of my last one to 'The Passage of Love'. Too positively gynaecological! I had a great effort to explain to her that if the Great GP could read something vulgar into a title, they would. I suggested she called it 'A Breast of the Times' and have done with it."

It was a relief to laugh, to reach out his hand, as if spontaneously, and touch her cheek. Her hand moved fast and caught his, and for a moment he felt the familiar hard shape of it in his palm before he pulled himself free.

"This is my local train, you know," he said, half ashamed of himself for worrying.

She drew back. "And you," she said quickly, to cover up whatever she might have felt at the rebuff. "How are you? Have you been well?"

He shrugged. "The usual complaints. I'm getting old, you know."

"Nonsense," she said. "You look as wonderful to me as you did when I first met you."

"You can't remember when you first met me," he said. He felt shy before her strength.

"Well, perhaps not the very first time – but I remember that first Christmas, when we went out for a drink on Christmas Eve, and you taught me the quickest way to get drunk." The memory, clear and fresh from her gleaming, iridescent mind, passed into his head and took root with all its implications of loss and betrayal. Such a mixture of hope and desolation swept over him that he felt for a moment sick, as if with vertigo.

"What do you do now?" he asked helplessly, forgetting the order of questions.

"Oh, I endure," she said shortly. "And you?"

"I work."

"I envy you that," she said. "That at least is a constructive thing."

"Everyone works," he said awkwardly. Her shining made him feel dull.

"No. Most people labour, only a few are lucky enough to work. I don't even labour – I merely endure."

"My work stopped being creative years ago," he said. "I'm just an ordinary hack musician – nothing to be proud of. I live in a dormitory town with the statutory wife and two kids, and I have the statutory unfulfilled dreams that I hardly even bother to dream any more." Why was he saying all this? It seemed to flow out from him as effortlessly as blood. Wounded, wounded. He cast about for her face, looked at her, then saw her.

"Oh Hamil," she said, on a dying cadence. "Was it for this we suffered? What happened to us in between?"

He looked at her, and then saw her, saw all that she had been in the years that had passed – but she was not pitiable. More resilient, always more resilient than him, she had retained some of that incandescence that had drawn all eyes to her, once, long ago, as she walked through the streets lit by her own private summer, from under whose sun she looked out on the world with a vast and shining patience. Even now, when all her sadness was in her face and lips, there was still that shining. He wanted to warm his hands at her.

"We got older, that's all," he said, with an effort to be calm, and he smiled.

"I don't believe that," she said. "We haven't changed so much. You're still all I want. God, how I want you!"

Desire flamed up in him instantly at the words, and his throat closed. He could make no possible reply. He saw it in her whole poise, and must have replied in some way, for she reached a hand towards him, began to move towards him; but a man, pushing out from the buffet car, looked at them curiously, and they both drew back. He fixed his eyes on her bare arms and concentrated on breathing slowly. He couldn't get off the train like this, with his lust like a banner before him. The air between them crackled with their mutual desire; he could smell it as he could smell lightning during a storm.

He had a vivid and gratifying vision of them slipping round the corner to the WC, locking the door, and of him having her there and then, all hungry hands and mouths, like teenagers. Instant sex! She had that power to arouse him. Would it have remained as potent if he had married her and lived with her all these years? Was it possible for any feeling other than boredom to outlast time? Were these thin and frugal years really so different from those he remembered as rich and heady and full of sex and mobility?

His erection was not fading, defying all his habitual morbidity, and he looked away from her, out of the window, and concentrated on breathing calmly. He became aware of the world hurtling past the windows and realised that the journey was not infinite, that he had little enough time to say to her all he would afterwards have wanted to say. But his mind had seized up, and he could not think what to ask. He fixed his mind on their past.

"How's Livilla?" he asked. He was interested to hear that his voice sounded quite normal, conversational.

She smiled abruptly.

"No one calls her that now but you."

"And you?"

"Oh yes, privately, to myself. But she's officially Gillian, and she's come to think of herself as Gillian too. Besides, she's at boarding-school now, and 'Livilla' would be a little of a burden. You know what savages children are."

"Boarding-school, eh? So Mother won in the end. Another little statuette for the mantelpiece."

"Livilla's that kind of child anyway."

"I don't believe it," Hamil said sharply. "None of us were. She made us that way."

"Are you so sure?" she asked, and she sounded tired. "I'm not. Oh, I believed it for years, of course, siding with you against your mother, trying to remove Frances and Ewan from her influence because you made me believe it was bad. But look at them! Or at least, at Frances – and remember, she's had the upbringing of Livilla far more than your mother. *She* only had her in the holidays. No, I think it's in the blood."

"She's yours, you know, your *blood*." He jerked the word out.

She shook her head. "I don't know. Perhaps I served my purpose in having her for the family. She belongs to you all more than me."

"All of us?" he asked bitterly. "What use was she to me? Look at me."

"I'm looking," she said, and he met her eyes again. Her incandescent joy at being with him – could it all be for him? Could he still, still arouse such a feeling in a young woman – for she seemed young, younger, perhaps, even than when she had been prisoner and nurse and gaoler to his brother. "I remember every moment we've had together," she said. "It was my life's function."

"Was? Is there no more to come?"

"I don't know." She could not, even now, name the evil god. She looked at him in the appeal of some last-ditch hope. "I often feel there must be. I seem to be so unfinished, living alone and purposelessly. Everything I've done seems to have broken off half-way, without coming to any sensible conclusion. Ewan, Livilla – you—"

"My father?" he asked. He had to, he couldn't help it. It seemed to him the ends of indecency were explored in that particular relationship.

"If you like," she shrugged. "You never did understand, did you?"

"No, I didn't."

"He was like a rock. You were all carved out of him – especially you, Hamil. I loved him and I loved all of you, but it wasn't sequential, or consequential. You were always my destination."

The memory of his father was inexpressibly painful to him. She saw that, and went on.

"And now here I am, still half-way through something, sawn in half," she said. They were silent a moment. Then she laid her hand on his arm. "Hamil, I have something to tell you. Perhaps I ought to have told you before, but I was afraid of what harm it might do. But I don't think it can hurt anyone now."

He was afraid. "Livia—"

"No, it's all right," she said quickly. "I just wanted to tell you, in case you had any doubt, that Livilla is yours. Your child."

He looked at her searchingly. It was the thing he had wanted to ask so many times, and been afraid to. It was at once a huge relief, and something he felt he had always known.

"You're sure?"

"There is no other possibility. There never was. Ewan knew, before he died, but no one else. That's why I had to keep it secret – for his sake, and hers, and the family's." She looked anxious. "If we had been able to be together—"

He knew she meant the three of them, as a family. The three of them – dear God! The golden vision flashed a moment before him and he turned away from it, unable to bear it. The other life he had not lived, the parallel universe which branched off that summer so many years ago when he had let her go.

She saw the movement and looked out of the window, to spare him. He looked too, seeing their journey, their time together, eaten almost away. "We're nearly there," he said fearfully.

"What now?" she asked. It came out a mere whisper.

"I don't know. I don't know." He lifted his hands in an incomplete gesture. It was the same question, never with any hope of an answer. It had always been the same question. "I only know I love you, and I don't think I can do anything about it."

"No?" Her voice quivered.

"It's Irene," he said helplessly. It was impossible to put into words all that that name implied, the colossal redundant fabric of his life that was implied by that small word. "And the children. It would take so much – organising. It would all be so messy. I don't think I could face the mess. I don't think we could survive that."

"We have a gift for survival, you and I," she said. "It needn't be messy. It only needs for you to walk away. Just as you are. Just as I am."

For a moment he thought about it.

"Stay on the train, you mean?"

She nodded. "Change at Norwich."

"And again at Peterborough – get the night train to Edinburgh."

"We'd be there early tomorrow; we could catch the first train across to Glasgow, have breakfast at the Cally, and then get the eight thirty to Fort William."

He had caught her drift. "Lunch at the George—"

"Then the steamer across to Skye—"

"The Outer Isles. We'd change our names – no one would know us."

"Mr and Mrs John Doe?"

He looked reproving. "Mrs and Mr Hamish McDonald."

"You'd hoe the beans. We'd have nine bean rows, and a hive for the honey-bee."

"Not a chance. *You'd* do the bean-hoeing. I'd be out in the boat."

She saw he was joking. She captured his eyes and said, "We could, you know."

They could, of course they could. For a moment everything faded out: the noise and stink of the crowded train, the sweating commuters, the black rattling howl past the windows – and with it all the world beyond the lighted stations, the world of semis and cars and kids and fish fingers and advertising, the working days and the dull, safe nights, the polite, conjugal bed and the desperate, desolate ache of each daily waking to it.

He smelt again the salt, iodine air and the bracing reek of seaweed, felt the soft and penetrating rain and heard the sea noise that is like a man's own heart beat, the sound he carries with him for ever that will lead him back at last to his own home. There was a place still that was quiet enough for that breathing sound to be heard, a place quiet with the quietness of a life that lives for itself, to provide only itself. Here he could be with her, sleep within the cradle of the wind to the long cries of seabirds; wake against the keep of her heart to the knowledge of another day in which they grew not older but more content, growing down into the earth like feeding trees.

"We could, you know," she said again. "I have a little capital.

It would be enough. You'd find your music again. There'd be no one to harm us."

He shook his head. "What about the others – Irene, and the children?"

"Think," she urged him. "Would she really miss you? Really? She has had all of you that she needs. And the children are old enough to understand. Almost grown up now. They could come and visit us in the summer, learn another set of values to measure against their own." She shrugged. "In any case, what have they to do with us? They have their own lives to live, as we have ours. There's only ever one chance, Hamil. How can you afford to throw this one life away? Don't die yet, don't try to die."

"For God's sake—"

"How much longer do you expect to live? *You might live forty years.*"

He drank from her eyes, and his mouth parted in fear and exhilaration like a pillion rider on a motor cycle. A sway of the train lilted her towards him, and she touched him lightly and swayed back. It was enough. He grabbed for her clumsily, pressed her to him. Ten years ago he would have kissed her, but gestures change as does language, and he only hugged her, pressing his face to her cheek, urging every surface of his body against her as if to protect her from some blast. He loved her so much. So close, so dear. *Hide in you – be here – don't leave me.*

"Livia," he said. "Livia. Don't – don't." He couldn't tell what it was she must not do, but she nodded in answer and pressed harder against him. Last chance? Of course it was his last chance. Yet with what sleight of hand did she invert the deep black hole of his failure into a modest mountain? In a few words she eliminated his colossal debt and filled his hands with grain. He had only to close his fingers, so that the grain should not slip through. Last chance. It was not a question of love, but knowledge. There was no thought or gesture concerning each other that they were not aware of. That was the "don't" – *don't be separate from me*. The classic divided one striving to be whole again, the classic cruel joke. *If you listen very carefully, you can hear the gods, laughing.*

The train braked and slowed, and the darkness was watered with the sickly and sulphurous lights of the town. Reality was drawing up alongside, and they were horribly, undeniably real, two middle-aged commuters clutching each other furtively in the corridor of a train and being eyed by a spotty boy soldier with the sardonic regard of a parrot. They drew apart, embarrassed, a little dazed.

Automatically he began to gather his belongings, and she watched him uncomprehendingly until the train screeched and juddered to a halt, startling her into action.

"Don't go," she said. He stared, aware of what he had been doing, of its implications, aware of the sickening weight of his life coming down on his back again. To draw away from it was like trying to draw air into his lungs through a blanket – the sheer effort filled him with nausea.

"I have to," he said. People were shoving up against them, anxious to join the sprint for the barrier and the car park. "She'll be waiting."

"Don't go." She held him with her urgency, but the pressure built up behind them as he hesitated, with the silent weight of snow against the door. The great wordless mass of homing workers, the leaden breath of their communal boredom, the urge of their collective obedience pressed against him, and like water breaking through a dam snatched him away. Looking back over his shoulder he saw her huddling against the carriage wall as they surged past her on to the platform.

He struggled out of the current and gained a still patch of platform, divided from her and the train by the flow. But even when the flow eased and he could have reached the train again, he knew it was too late, and he stood still, numb with despair, as the doors were slammed shut, and the train began to move.

She was at the window, and it seemed for a very long time they looked at each other as the bond of sight was slowly stretched, drawing them apart. She said, not shouting but speaking quite distinctly, "I shall be on the same train tomorrow," and he nodded. His vision was blurring with the effort and she was invisible to him long before she was out of sight.

Epilogue

Irene heard the car long before it reached the turning – at the same time as Judy. The dog's movement caught her eye, and she turned her head towards her. Judy's eyes were glowing with pleasure and she was beating her tail softly on the floor.

How different their reaction, Irene thought. How ironic. Judy greeted the car with anticipatory pleasure, the long pleasure of having all her humans together again in one place. Her first action after greeting him would be to put her head down with a sigh and go to sleep.

For Irene the reaction to the noise was a jerk of apprehension. *How will he be*? It seemed to her suddenly terrible that she, his wife, should be afraid of his coming home, so that her heart would sink when the car stopped in front of the house, and she would wait, crackling with tension, during that known pause, the time it took him to get out of the car and walk to the door.

Then there would be the internal noise of the door being opened, and another pause while he took off his coat, picked up the post from the hall table and flicked through it. Then he would come in to her, and there would be that sickening big-dipper moment when the door would open and she would force herself to look at him and see how much he had drunk and what mood he was in.

It wasn't that he would come in reeling and belching like a comedian, or cursing and violent – of course not; though she, who had never lived with a drunkard, sometimes thought it might be better so. When he had drunk a lot, he talked: obscure, convoluted, erudite stuff that she didn't understand, and she would feel humiliated by her stupidity as she stumbled and fumbled after his meaning, and take the gleam in his eye for sarcasm or contempt.

Sometimes he would have drunk little, and he would come in tired, politely indifferent to her. "Hello darling, had a good day?"

"Oh, so-so."

"Any news?"

"No, nothing."

"Boys in OK?"

"Yes, they're fine."

And he would sit down to read his letters, and she would nervously offer him tea, coffee, a milk drink, something to eat. She wanted, in the relief of the moment, to give him things, to feed and comfort him, to be a wife to him as she had seen her mother be a wife to her father. Her mother's function had always been largely nutritional. To Irene, kindness and food were inextricably linked.

But he would never take anything from her. He would refuse with that same neutral politeness, as if he was hardly aware of her. Taut and vibrating with conversation she would watch him reading his mail and fondling Judy's eager head; waiting for an opening. He would look up in the end, his eyes travelling towards her and then just missing at the last moment. To the back of her chair or the standard lamp he would address himself – she had to retrieve his remarks like a ball-boy in a grown-ups' tennis game. "Why don't you go on up to bed? I'll be up in a minute. I'll just read this and take Judy out and then I'll be up."

Of course, she always went. Avoidance of trouble became a reflex action, like telling children to be careful. She would go up to bed and, sitting at the dressing table, would find she was trembling. A whole day, from not seeing him off in the morning to the long wait through the evening, had built up to that moment when he came in through the sitting room door. And nothing had happened. She felt quite sick with the pent-up effort. They had made no pigeon-step forward, they were exactly where they had been the night before.

Talk to him? But it was one of the rules that she should be asleep when he came up from walking Judy. Even if she had the will to break the rules for her own sake, the sight of him, stooped with weariness, taking off his clothes as if they were heavy with water, made her desist out of pity. He fell into bed and slept instantly, snoring heavily in his first, dead sleep. After ten minutes or so he would turn on to his side and sleep quietly, and she would lie close, not quite touching him, while her mind gabbled through the dark hours.

That was when he came home sober. Not better, but easier, because no effort was required of her, only obedience to the pattern which had been devised to protect him from discovery. Recently she had begun to realise that there was probably a protection for her, too, implicit in that silence. Under that camouflage net there were two beasts sharing a den and not harming each other, beasts of different species. Their marriage had been no more than that, though it had taken her all these years to realise it.

In the first year of their marriage he had been kind and attentive, and they had had a feverish kind of sex-love. But that, like everything else, had slipped after a while into a routine, while the kindness had turned into polite indifference by such imperceptible stages that she had not noticed the change. In the middle years she had believed their marriage was good, had seen their lack of conflict as harmony. Only of late had she realised how skilfully he had hidden himself from her. What had their union been, after all? She didn't know why he had married her. She didn't know any of the whys about him.

Her mother came into her mind, clear and sharp like a good photograph, her dear, irreplaceable mother.

"Are you sure you want to marry him? You seem only to have known him for a very little time."

"I've known him all my life, Mother. That's how I feel, anyway. I know it hasn't been long in actual time, but time isn't important, is it?"

"But does he love you?"

"Of course he does. Why else would he want to marry me?"

Why else indeed? So confident, that young Irene, of what she knew. Mother, so gently puzzled. Irene, dizzy with love, overwhelmed with passion. She should have suspected, that plump, healthy, tennis-playing young Irene, that Hamil was something else again. She had met his family. She knew all about breeding – dogs, cats and rabbits, guinea-pigs and hamsters. She should have known that one pup in the litter could not be so absolutely different from the rest.

"My family", he had said, distantly and reprovingly, as if they were something unfortunate left on his doorstep. "My family", and the "my" detached them firmly from him: he was not one of them, not like them at all. And she had believed it – or rather, had accepted it, not thought about it at all; had married him, and believed she knew him.

But that blood was in him. Inexorably it called him back; that strange, ancient, pagan tree had its roots twisting right down into his soul.

She had taken to watching the children covertly for signs of that blood in them. Fergus and Francis – so close they were often mistaken for twins, spoken of always in a pair, "Fergie and Francey", as one spoke of a married couple. But lately they were not so twinlike as they had been. The black roots worked on, deeper into the ground. Hadn't there, recently, been a growing strangeness about Francey? That business a year ago about becoming a vegetarian – and he had stuck to it, had not eaten meat since, enormous extra work and worry for her. And then, beginning at Christmas, that sudden fever of religion. As a family they had always gone to church, but suddenly Francey was spending hours at prayer, reading things, slipping off at odd hours to light candles and sit in silent contemplation of Our

Lady. It wasn't natural in a boy his age. Too much religion at that age could so easily turn into weirdness.

Hamil could have talked to him about it – but Hamil was never there, and was as politely inaccessible to the children as he was to her. So what could she do? It was only one of the things she needed him for. But he came home less and less, and was more elusive when he did come. She was in terror that he would one day announce that he was leaving, and just go. If she could have absolute warning of this, she would leave him first, for there would be nothing worse than being the one to be left. But of course, she couldn't know it for certain until it happened, and then it would be too late. She could never leave him for her own sake, for one glimpse of the yawning void of her life without him put it beyond the last resort, like death.

So every night she waited, strung up on the length of the day, on her fitful anxiety, on the increasing depth of the silence – she could no longer quite touch the bottom. Waiting for Hamil to come home and determine – or not determine – the shape of her life. Sometimes, in the last half-hour before she could reasonably expect him, she would play out that last scene in her mind: visualise his expression as he said it, imagine the exact words, and plan her own replies, varying from the dignified silence to the impassioned plea. Over and again she would play the scene, make some kind of a part for herself, until she was so exhausted with it she would almost rather provoke it than live another night and day with its menace.

Almost. When the moment came, she was always glad enough to get off lightly. So now she listened to the car stopping outside and hoped they might go to bed again with nothing determined – that they might preserve this perilous status quo, because she didn't want to know about the alternative.

Judy's head went up. They both froze, listening. The silence sang around them, and Irene's nerves shredded. The moment extended and extended until she knew there must be something wrong, that the known pause had passed two or three times over. Judy whined softly, and then got up and padded over to the door, dropping her muzzle to the gap below it as if it might tell her something her ears could not.

"He's probably fiddling with the car," she told the dog, and her voice startled her, sounding too loud in the straining silence. Judy looked up and swung her tail politely, but her heart was outside in the darkness. She whined again. A sudden terror seized Irene, that he had had a heart attack out there in the car, and was sitting slumped over the wheel, cooling as the engine cooled. She felt a sweat break out under her arms. Another minute went past and she knew she should go out and see what was wrong. Suppose he was not dead, but dying, needing help?

She didn't move. Another minute. And then at last the sound of the key in the door. Judy sang, her nose pressed to the gap under the door through which his presence came to her in great cordial draughts. How good to love as simply as that, and to have the love reciprocated. His hand on her head as he came in would be enough for her – and she would get it.

The door opened sharply and Judy shuffled backwards to avoid being hit. *I shall say something, lightly, about his being so long. I shall say, "I thought you'd had a heart attack."*

And then Hamil was in the doorway. His eyes were inflamed, as if he had been crying, and there was that expression on his face that she had never been able to imagine, however often she played out the last scene in her mind. It was the end. Her heart stood aside from her, for she could read it in his face.

Irene put her two hands together in her lap and looked up at him wordlessly. Her mind shelled another. One, hurt past all helping, lay in a pool of blood, kicking slowly with the last of its life. The other skirted it and asked quite calmly and logically what would happen to Judy? She couldn't imagine him taking her, but Judy would pine without him. Irene had never been more than a poor substitute to the dog. Judy would never be able to understand his desertion, would wait with her nose pressed to the door until her heart broke.

The moment had passed and another taken its place, and even before he spoke Irene knew that the worst was over and that she would never again feel pain or grief as bad as that. She gathered herself into her hands in readiness, and then, as her own anguish passed from her, she saw that he was in trouble, that he had, indeed, been crying. Hardly knowing what she did, she stood up and offered him her chair, and taking the gesture for what it was, not noticing its absurdity, he sat down.

Judy pressed forward and thrust her face into his hands, her tail swinging so hard it twitched her rump from side to side. Hamil's hands moved automatically, closing over Judy's head, pulling her ears, caressing. Judy's eyes shone with ecstasy: her world was preserved intact and her life fulfilled for a little longer.

Fear had passed from Irene. She saw that he was at the end of a very long, frayed tether. He looked exhausted. She had never seen anyone so near to being broken, and knew she must be the one to be strong. She stood firm and asked, "What's wrong?"

After a long moment he said, "I can't go on." He looked up at her to see if she understood. She nodded, almost impatiently, as if to say, "Well, I know *that.*"

How could he explain the anguish? He put his hands to his head, and Judy, deprived, nudged up after them. "I just can't go on with this."

"What's happened?" Irene asked. "You were so long out there I thought you'd had a heart attack and died. What were you doing?"

He looked at her, and folded the tentative opening of his mind back in on itself. Impossible to tell her everything that had passed, was still passing, through his brain: the longing, the grief, the appalling need. Of course she would not understand. But she would want the facts, of course; the facts. Well, he owed her that much, perhaps owed her a justification for all the years he should not have been married to her. She was his ultimate failure; the structure of which she was part was the monument to his failure, to the slow death of the best part of him.

Should he alone take the blame for marrying her? Had she not married him at least as dishonestly? She had wanted him because he had fitted her idea of a romantic hero. She had never wanted to know what he was really like, had never cared for him at all as long as he played his part as husband and provider.

And he had married her because she was not like his mother or his sisters, those involuted women who had twisted at his soul since his childhood. He had married her thinking, perhaps subconsciously, that her simplicity was a thing that could absorb his complexity. But of course it didn't work that way. Even to conceive of complexity was beyond her. If ever he had given her a true reason for something, she had disregarded it as camouflage, had determined a hidden simple reason to which she could simply react.

And, of course, she would never understand what he meant by failure. To her success was tangible: he had a good job, a nice house, two clean polite children. If he spoke of metaphysical failure, she would disregard it as a fatuous excuse, and look for the "real" reason. Well, then, he would give her one. He would give her a tangible fact and let her think what she would. He looked up at her in anguish, but they would part on a lie, as they had lived.

She drew in her breath sharply, and dropped to her haunches beside him, an impetuous movement unlike her. She fumbled for one of his hands. Judy turned her nose from one of them to the other, not knowing which to love.

"I wish," Irene said, and her voice trembled, "you could ever have told me what was wrong. Why are you so unhappy? Were you crying, out there in the car? Oh Hamil, what's happened?"

I wish you could ever have told me? Had she, then, ever known there was anything to tell? He looked searchingly at her, for had she been that kind of Irene, there might never have been a problem. What did she mean? He tried to see in, but her face, too familiar now, was opaque to him.

No, there was no possibility of her understanding. He had to give her what she wanted, give her as little as possible, keep the rest. She must be told something, but let it be only a fact, for facts are unimportant, facts don't touch you where you live.

"I met someone on the train," he said at last. Would she take it? He looked at her in hope, a strategy forming. There was a commonplace scene they could play out that might leave them both, though for different reasons, the dignity they needed to survive afterwards. The precedents were there: let her think of him as just a middle-aged man running off with a dolly bird, and they might both escape with their souls intact. It was kinder that way, to both of them.

Irene, holding his hand in that surprisingly masculine, comforting way, asked, "Who was it?"

"An old flame," he said with an attempt at an embarrassed smile. "I couldn't help it. These things creep up on you. I can hardly expect you to forgive me, but it just happened. One can't help falling in love. I hadn't thought about her for ages, didn't expect to see her again, but there she was, completely by chance – the most extraordinary thing – almost an act of God, you might say." He spun the words industriously, for kindness, weaving in colour for her sake, so that she might believe it and live.

Irene looked at him steadily, waiting; but when he went on, talking, talking as if she were an idiot, she dropped his hand and stood up. "What a liar you are," she said in disgust. He stopped abruptly. She walked away a few steps and then came back, shaking with anger. "You think I'm a complete fool, don't you? You haven't even enough respect for me to tell me the truth."

"Irene, don't," he said. She was like a child blundering into danger.

"I could have loved you, comforted you even – but you give Judy more of yourself than you ever gave me."

"But you never wanted me," Hamil said. He could not believe that all these years he had been wrong, for that would have implied such wasted opportunity that he could not have endured the remorse.

"What do you know about what I want?"

"There are things better not to ask. Believe me."

She waved a hand, brushing aside the evasion of words. She would have it out now. Day after day the silence had deepened, and now she struck out, to swim as far as she could before she drowned.

"Who did you meet?" she demanded. "Who was it?"

He outstared her a moment, as though he would still refuse to tell her. Then he said, "Olivia. It was Olivia."

She hardly knew what she had expected, but when the answer came it had the inevitability of a blow falling for the second time on the same place. The pain was sickening. And she had thought only minutes ago that she was over the worst! A lifetime of suspicions and fears which she had suppressed or argued herself out of because they were too terrible to contemplate were hauled out now into plain view; a vast and intricate structure, whose multiple ramifications she seemed to grasp now at last in one shocked glance.

He was right – there were things better not to know. The reality was worse, far worse, than her imaginings. She saw it in his face, that here was something that mattered to him on a level where she had never existed, on a scale against which the whole of her life with him was a grain of sand to a mountain. She couldn't comprehend what that woman had meant to him. She stepped back a pace from his pain, as one might recoil instinctively from an accident.

The pause had been brief in real time, but she seemed to be speaking from the other end of the universe. "I suppose I should have known," she said. "Olivia."

Hamil flinched at the sound of her name spoken by Irene's voice, afraid of anything touching that cool place in his mind where she grew like a tree, the undefiled.

"Known what? What could you know?"

"I was only ever a substitute for her, wasn't I?"

"You were never a substitute," he said helplessly.

There was a silence between them, while his hands went on mechanically stroking the dog, and the seconds moved them breath by breath away from that moment of horrible revelation and into an unknown country.

"And what now?" Irene said at last.

What now indeed? There were no rules of engagement from this place onwards. "I don't know," he said.

"Do you think it could ever work out in real life? If you do, you're a fool."

"Perhaps," he said. Hadn't he thought the same thing himself? Hadn't *she* said – on some other occasion, a lifetime ago – "I am not real to you"? Could he spare the time either to doubt or to experiment? The end was nearer than the beginning – was that a reason to move, or a reason to stay still? He didn't know. How could he decide? He was afraid of everything – of failure most of all. "Perhaps nothing will happen," he said. *Happen. Let things happen. Don't make a decision which might be wrong. If you stay still enough, God decides for you.*

Irene watched him, wearily, and saw the awful possibility there to hand – saw it at the exact moment it occurred to him – that they might let it go and return to their former life. They could cover up and say nothing, regard this as a mere letting-off of steam. Hamil, she knew, would always rather not make decisions. The great weight of snow had built up against the door, and the door had creaked, but it had held. So tempting, so tempting. *How many more years?* So many years behind them, and a maze built up in which they could elude each other, given luck, for ever.

For the rest of her life, knowing what he had always wanted, watching him pour his love out on the dog? There was some kind of truth in her yet that would not lie down, a wholeness he had never touched that breathed clean air and had contempt for him.

She pushed aside the weariness and the temptation. She looked into his confusion and saw only her own clear path.

"You were right," she said. "You can't go on like this. You must decide what you will do."

She stopped speaking. A silence followed, nothing to be heard but the two-tone voice of a diesel, the last train going home, calling faintly through the blackness beyond the windows.